'Hey,' he said, curiously tender.

'I'm sorry,' she whispered as the tears began to run unchecked down her face. 'It was so awful up there, so wet and wild...and...and so lonely...' She shook her head in distress, unable to blot out the pictures that filled her head.

Without a word Casey stepped forward, put his arms around her and held her close. It felt safe, warm and secure in the shelter of his arms, and at that moment, if she'd been asked, Adele quite easily could have said that she was happy to stay there indefinitely. But gradually, inevitably, common sense returned.

'I'm sorry,' she muttered. 'That was very unprofessional of me.'

'Not at all.' He didn't release her, just moved back a bit so he could look into her face again while keeping his arms around her. He really should let her go, she thought, albeit half-heartedly, but he didn't.

Laura MacDonald lives on the Isle of Wight and is married with a grown-up family. She has enjoyed writing fiction since she was a child and for several years she worked for members of the medical profession, both in pharmacy and in general practice. Her daughter is a nurse and has helped with the research for Laura's medical stories.

Recent titles by the same author:

MEDIC ON APPROVAL
THE SURGEON'S DILEMMA
A VERY TENDER PRACTICE
DR PRESTON'S DAUGHTER

POLICE DOCTOR

BY
LAURA MacDONALD

All the characters in this book have no existence outside the imagination of the author, and have no relation whatsoever to anyone bearing the same name or names. They are not even distantly inspired by any individual known or unknown to the author, and all the incidents are pure invention.

First published in Great Britain 2002
Harlequin Mills & Boon Limited,
Eton House, 18-24 Paradise Road, Richmond, Surrey TW9 1SR

© Laura MacDonald 2002

ISBN 0 263 83103 5

Set in Times Roman 10½ on 12 pt.
03-1102-50961

Printed and bound in Spain
by Litografia Rosés, S.A., Barcelona

CHAPTER ONE

'ADELE, it's good to see you again.' Edward Fletcher stood up, came round his desk and, instead of shaking her hand, which she had expected him to do, kissed her warmly on the cheek. 'Please, do come in and sit down.' The kindly GP indicated a chair alongside his desk. Feeling rather like a cross between one of his patients and some long-lost niece, Adele sat down.

'Did you have a good journey?' Edward asked as he resumed his own seat.

'Yes, it wasn't too bad at all once I got onto the M6.'

'Well, I hope you're going to be happy with us all here in Stourborne Abbas.'

'I'm sure I will be,' Adele replied, looking round at Edward's consulting room as she spoke. She could still hardly believe that she was here, that she'd actually left the familiar world of her home town of Chester and her life as a hospital doctor and started out on the road to becoming a GP.

'Adele, before we go any further I have to tell you that there are one or two things that have changed since you came for your interview.' Suddenly Edward's affable expression had become serious and Adele felt a twinge of unease.

'What sort of things?' she asked.

'Well, for a start, unfortunately I've been diagnosed with angina and high blood pressure which has meant I've had to reduce my workload.'

'I'm sorry to hear that,' said Adele slowly. 'Does this

5

mean my coming here has caused problems?' She looked at Edward and could see now that he did indeed look tired and rather drawn.

'Not really.' He shook his head. 'But I'm afraid that what it does mean is that I am no longer able to be your trainer. Don't worry,' he added when he saw her look of alarm, 'it isn't going to be as much of a problem as you might think. My partner, Casey, has agreed to take over. Now, Casey wasn't at your interview—he was taking a three-month sabbatical at the time.'

'So is he happy with this new arrangement?' asked Adele dubiously.

'Oh, yes. In fact, it was he who suggested it.'

'Really?' Adele raised her eyebrows in surprise.

'Yes, but he does also happen to be my own GP and having just told me to slow down...'

'He didn't have a lot of choice—is that what you're saying?'

'Something like that.' Edward laughed, seeming to like her direct manner. Growing serious again, he said, 'But you mustn't worry, Adele, your training year isn't in any jeopardy at all. Apart from the fact that it won't be me who is your trainer everything else is as it stood at your interview and your flat is available upstairs. And there is also just one thing that I think might even be to your advantage.'

'Oh?' said Adele, trying to show some enthusiasm. Suddenly she felt rather flat, as if her arrival at the practice in Stourborne Abbas was some dreadful sort of anticlimax. 'And what is that?'

'At your interview you said that you were interested in forensics and police work.'

'Yes, that's right,' Adele agreed. 'I've always felt that's an area I might like to explore further in the future.'

'Well, Casey happens to be the police surgeon for Stourborne Abbas.'

'Really?' Suddenly there seemed possibilities in this new arrangement, which, if she was honest, had thrown her slightly. She had prepared herself to spend a year under the tuition and guidance of this kind and easygoing man and now it seemed that crucial year was to be spent with a man she hadn't even met. 'Tell me,' she said looking up, her gaze meeting that of Edward's, 'what is Casey's surname?'

Edward chuckled. 'Casey is his surname,' he said. 'He likes it that way,' he added when he saw her look of surprise. 'Now,' he went on briskly, 'back to basics.' Opening a drawer in his desk, he took out a set of keys and handed them to her. 'These are the keys to your flat,' he said, adding as an afterthought, 'What have you done with your car?'

'It's on the forecourt,' Adele replied. 'Is that all right?' she added.

'Yes, but I suggest you bring it round to the rear of the building. There's a small car park round there reserved just for the doctors. When you've done that I'll get one of the girls to take you upstairs to your flat. I'd do it myself but...' he pulled a face '...stairs and I don't seem terribly compatible these days.'

Moments later Adele was back in her car and reversing out of the forecourt in front of Woolverton House—Stourborne Abbas's medical centre. It was a large house, over two hundred years old and occupying a prime position in the high street of the busy market town. The house had, in its time, as Adele had already found out, been the family home of a wealthy cloth merchant, a small private school for the children of gentlefolk and for a long period of time a hotel, but more recently had been taken over by the local group practice as its health centre.

Following Edward's instructions, Adele turned the car into an entrance to the right of the building, driving beneath an archway and into a cobbled courtyard where she found three cars already parked and spaces for three more. Carefully she reversed into one of the spaces—it took some manoeuvering as the space was tight but at last, with a sigh of relief, she was able to switch off her engine. Leaning forward, she looked up at the old, mews-type buildings with their gables and attics under the eaves that formed the rear of the house, and just for a moment found herself wondering about the people who had lived there in times gone by, imagining the merchant's children playing in the courtyard or the servants going about their daily tasks. History was one of Adele's passions and it was Woolverton House itself that had been the deciding factor in her reaching her decision to come to Stourborne Abbas for this crucial year of her training.

Opening the car door, she had just stepped out onto the cobbles when she jumped as a sudden roar filled the air, shattering the peace of the quiet courtyard as a large, powerful motorbike swept under the archway, circled then drove into the space opposite Adele. For a moment she felt irritated that her musings of the past had been so violently interrupted by such an acute reminder of the modern world and she found herself glaring indignantly at the rider. Clad almost entirely in black leather, his face— at least, Adele presumed it was a he, there seemed little chance that the powerful figure before her could belong to a woman—was hidden behind the visor of a shiny black crash helmet. Quite suddenly and irrationally her irritability spilled over. Later she was to wonder exactly why, but at the time it had been nothing more than the fact that he had disturbed her moment of peace or maybe it had been something to do with his attitude. First he surveyed her from astride his machine and then as he dismounted, the action in itself suggested an arrogance, which touched a raw nerve.

'You can't park there,' she stated flatly, her voice rising slightly. 'It's reserved for doctors' cars.'

Carefully he unfastened his crash helmet and removed it, shaking his head slightly as he did so, and Adele found herself looking into a pair of eyes that were neither entirely grey nor green but somewhere in between, their expression unreadable as he stared at her, not exactly hostile, just indefinable, which did little to relieve the jangling of her nerves. His hair was dark, cropped close to his head, his features rugged, not handsome, maybe attractive to a certain kind of woman but not handsome, certainly not handsome like Nigel.

But she mustn't think of Nigel now, she told herself firmly, she mustn't think about Nigel at all, it was too dangerous for that was a road that led to despair and depression. Nigel had classical good looks with his blue eyes and fair skin, his blond hair and aristocratic features and the man before her resembled a bandit from a bad Hollywood movie. Why, he even had a scar on his face which ran from the centre of his left eyebrow to the edge of his jaw, acquired, no doubt, in some drunken brawl. She found herself imagining the body beneath the black leathers to be covered in tattoos and expected, as he unfastened the collar of his jacket, to catch the gleam of gold from at least one earring. But there was none and as, without speaking, he removed his gauntlets and unzipped his jacket it was obvious he intended disregarding Adele and staying where he was.

'Did you hear what I said?' she demanded.

'Yes,' he replied calmly, 'you said these spaces were reserved for doctors' cars, in which case I could question what *you* are doing parked there.' He glanced beyond her towards her car as he spoke.

'I am a doctor.' She tilted her chin defiantly, still irritated by the man's whole demeanour.

'Really?' His tone held a suggestion that he doubted the fact. 'I don't think we've met.'

Something in his manner compelled Adele to answer. 'I'm Dr Brooks,' she said, as haughtily as she could, 'Adele Brooks.' She paused and when he still didn't offer any information as to his identity, in the same tone she said, 'And you are?'

'I also am a doctor,' he stated quietly. 'The name's Casey.'

She felt such a fool, but how could she have known that this man who had managed to irritate her for no apparent reason and in such a short space of time was not only one of the partners but also the man who was now to be her trainer for the next year?

'I'm sorry,' she found herself muttering, 'I didn't think you were a doctor. You don't look like a doctor...' she added in her defence.

'And what are doctors supposed to look like?' There was a mocking expression in Casey's eyes now, which only served to irritate Adele even further.

'Well, I don't know too many who wear black leathers or who ride high-powered motorbikes,' she retorted.

'What you're saying is that the ones you know drive BMWs or Volvos and wear tweed jackets, is that right?'

'Something like that, yes.' Adele nodded, wishing she could escape from this man whose stare was beginning to make her feel very uncomfortable.

'I find a motorbike more practical for negotiating traffic

and leather is the only sure protection against the elements or sudden contact with the tarmac. I use the practice Land Rover on occasion…' he nodded towards the large vehicle in one corner of the courtyard '…but I much prefer the freedom of the bike.' He paused, his gaze briefly wandering over her, seemingly taking in every detail of her appearance, from her slender figure in the black suit she had chosen to wear because she had fondly believed it might create the right impression on her first day to her long dark hair and the scarlet ribbed top that matched her lipstick. 'So you're Adele Brooks,' he said thoughtfully, and there was no way of telling whether he approved of what he saw or not. Not giving her a chance to answer, he carried on, 'Have you seen Edward yet?'

'I have.' She paused. 'It was he who told me to come and park here,' she added quickly.

'Did he also tell you about the new arrangements?'

Adele nodded, wondering in that instant quite how she was going to endure working for a whole year with this man who, as far as she could tell on such short acquaintance, was as different from Edward Fletcher as it was possible to be.

'Where's your luggage?' He leaned sideways and looked at the boot of her car.

Without a word she turned and walked to the rear of the car, unlocked the boot and began dragging out one of her two large suitcases.

'Let me do that.' He was suddenly beside her, his leather-clad figure alarmingly close in the restricted space between the car and the wall.

'It's all right, I can manage…' she began, but he ignored her, lifting out the second suitcase and setting it briefly down on the ground before picking up both cases and heading for a doorway on the far side of the courtyard, leaving Adele to scoop up the rest of her belongings and follow him. He kicked open the door and disappeared into a long dark passage at the end of which Adele realised he had turned and was climbing a staircase. He only spoke once and that was when they reached the first landing and he looked briefly over his shoulder. 'Did you see your flat when you came for your interview?'

'No. The previous occupant was asleep at the time but I did see the flat that belongs to one of the practice nurses and I was told it's very similar to the one I would have.'

He was silent until they reached the second floor. A corridor stretched out before them but they walked barely half its length before he stopped before a closed door and set down the cases. 'Did Edward give you your keys?' he asked, as if it had only just occurred to him.

'Yes.' Adele would have unlocked the door herself but he took the keys from her and inserted one of them in the lock, pushed open the door then picked up the cases once more and preceded Adele into the room.

Her first impression was one of light, the warm sunlight of the September afternoon that spilled into the room from the tall, sash-cord windows highlighting the sheen on the polished wooden floor.

'You know it's only a studio flat?' He turned towards her after setting the cases down.

'Yes, but I decided as it was just for a year I could probably cope with that.'

'It does have its own bathroom and kitchen.' He crossed the room in his slow, unhurried way and opened a door to which presumably had once been a large bedroom but which now had been converted to accommodate the facilities he had just mentioned. Following him, Adele allowed herself a brief look around and was satisfied by what she saw. 'Is Penny still a neighbour?' she asked at last. Penny

Rudge was the practice nurse whom Adele had met at her interview and whose flat she had seen.

He nodded. 'She is. We've adopted a new policy with these apartments—above the shop so to speak. We now only rent them out to members of staff.'

'Was that not the case before?'

'No, and the previous occupant of this flat turned out to be a bit of a troublemaker. She had to go in the end.'

'Really?' Adele raised her eyebrows.

'I hope you won't be a troublemaker, Dr Brooks.'

It was such an unexpected comment to make that Adele found herself swinging round to protest, then having to bite back her ready retort as she saw the wry smile that hovered around the corners of his mouth and realised that he wasn't serious. 'It depends,' she said lightly, 'on the way I'm treated as to whether or not I make trouble. If I'm treated well I'm the most easygoing person in the world, but if anyone treats me badly, believe me, Dr Casey, I'm more than capable of making trouble.'

'Casey,' he said with a frown.

'Sorry?'

'You said Dr Casey.'

'Isn't that your name?'

'I prefer plain Casey,' he replied.

'As you wish.' She shrugged.

'I'll leave you to get yourself sorted out,' he said. 'You'd better give one of us a shout if there's anything you want.'

'What about food?' Adele glanced around.

'I'm afraid we don't run to room service here.' The mocking expression was back in those rather curious eyes of his and Adele felt herself flush.

'I wasn't suggesting that,' she protested. 'What I meant

was that presumably there's somewhere I can buy something.'

'There's a small supermarket just down the high street, but—'

'That'll be fine, thanks,' she replied crisply, cutting him short. Suddenly she wanted him to go. She wanted to be alone to explore her flat and settle herself down into what was, after all, going to be her home for the next year. And she wanted to do it well away from the gaze of this man who for the moment she didn't really know quite how to take.

'I'll leave you to it, then.' He strolled to the door then stopped and looked back. 'You'll be ready to start tomorrow?'

It was barely a question, rather, Adele felt, an instruction. 'Of course,' she murmured coolly. Unexpectedly, his features softened into the semblance of something that could almost, but not quite, have passed as a smile, and she felt obliged to say, 'Thank you for bringing my cases up.'

'No problem,' he replied, and then ruined it by saying, 'Eight-thirty sharp in the morning. Don't be late—I can't abide unpunctuality.' Then he was gone out of the flat, closing the door behind him and leaving Adele standing in the middle of the room with her belongings at her feet.

Finally able to relax, she looked around the room. It was a very large room, complete with a sofa-bed in a pale mustard colour strewn with huge, comfy-looking cushions. The décor looked fresh, as if it had all recently been painted, with light, wheat-coloured walls, white paintwork and with long, turquoise, muslin curtains that drifted gently in the breeze from the open window. There were a few ornaments, a large vase in the fireplace filled with twigs, seedpods and twisted pieces of tree bark and on the walls

a couple of watercolour prints of local views. There were
adequate cupboards, drawers and wardrobe space for her
belongings and the kitchen and bathroom, though basic,
were spotlessly clean and rather disappointingly modern.
She would quite have liked to have found an old Victorian
claw-foot bath in a house such as this. The rooms them-
selves were full of character with little nooks and crannies,
and between the main room and the bathroom an unexpected window set with tiny panes of stained glass and
with a deep sill on which someone had thoughtfully placed
a glass bowl of fragrantly scented pot-pourri.

She unpacked her clothes and hung them up in the vast
wardrobe then took a shower and was just drying her hair
when she heard a tap on her door.

'Who is it?' she called, switching off her hair-dryer and
making up her mind that if it was Dr Casey or whatever
he called himself she would say she was changing.

'It's Penny. Penny Rudge.'

'Oh, Penny.' Scrambling to her feet, Adele crossed the
room and pulled open the door.

'Hi Adele. Welcome to Woolverton House!' Short,
round and blonde with large, expressive brown eyes,
Penny Rudge stood on the threshold, a bottle of wine
clasped in one hand, a bunch of flowers in her arms and
a white square box in her other hand.

'Penny, lovely to see you again. Come in, please.' Adele
smiled as she stood back to allow Penny to enter the room.

'These are for you—the flowers and wine are from the
rest of the staff and this is from me.' As she spoke she
thrust the white box into Adele's hands.

'Oh, how kind.' Adele lifted the lid and peeped into the
box. 'Wow, that looks wonderful!'

'It's lemon custard tart—made by the bakery next door

and absolutely scrummy. Thought you might be in need of a little spirit-raiser.'

'Oh, thank you…you're so kind. And what lovely flowers! I must see if I can find a vase for them. Please, do come in and sit down.'

'I'm glad Rosie cleaned this place up,' said Penny as she perched on the edge of the sofa and looked around her while Adele hurried into the kitchen.

'Who's Rosie?' called Adele.

'The surgery cleaner, she's a real treasure.'

'So does she clean the flats as well as the surgery?' asked Adele as she came back into the room, a vase full of water in one hand and two wineglasses in the other.

'She will if you come to some agreement with her. This flat was in a bit of a mess after the last occupant left—I'm just glad it's cleaned up all right.'

'I understand there was a bit of trouble with the last tenant,' said Adele as she unwrapped the flowers—yellow rosebuds and amber carnations—and began placing them in the vase.

'You could say that.' Penny pulled a face then, changing the subject, she said, 'Have you seen Dr Fletcher yet?'

'Yes, I saw him when I arrived.'

'How did you find him?'

Adele looked up. 'Well, I was shocked to learn about his heart problems.'

'He's been working far too hard.'

'Hence the reason he's unable to be my trainer.' Lifting the vase, Adele placed it in the sunlight on a low coffee-table by the window. 'There,' she said, 'they look lovely there. Now, I'll cut this tart and pour some wine. You will join me, won't you? A celebration wouldn't be any fun at all on my own.'

'Absolutely,' said Penny with a sigh. 'Any excuse, that's

what I say.' She was silent while Adele went back to the kitchen and found a bottle-opener, plates, a knife and two forks. When Adele returned and opened the bottle of wine, Penny said, 'Are you very disappointed—about Dr Fletcher, I mean?'

Adele paused, the bottle poised over a glass and considered. 'Well, yes,' she said at last, 'I suppose I am. I really took to him when I met him at the interview and in the meantime I suppose I had envisaged what it would be like working alongside him for the next year.'

'I know, he's a real sweetie, but you mustn't be too upset.' Penny took the glass of wine that Adele held out to her. 'Casey is just as good. Cheers!' She lifted her glass.

'Yes, cheers!' Adele lifted her own glass then took a sip. The wine was extremely good. It was on the tip of her tongue to ask whether Dr Casey was also a sweetie but it seemed such a ludicrous question and so obviously not the case that she remained silent. Instead, she set her glass down and set about cutting the lemon custard tart.

'Where is it you've come from?' asked Penny as she settled herself more comfortably on the sofa. 'You probably did tell me before but I can't remember.'

'Chester.' Adele passed a plate across the table then sat down on the rug in front of the fireplace with her own plate.

'That's right, I remember now.' Penny nodded. 'Well, you may find this practice very different from your hospital work but they're a pretty good bunch to work with. We have our ups and downs, same as any place of work, but on the whole we all get on OK. I hope you'll be happy here, Adele.' Her face broke into a wide smile.

'Thanks, Penny, I'm sure I will. I must say I'm glad you're living in the building as well.' She paused. 'You were absolutely right about this tart—it's really delicious.'

'I know.' Penny grinned. 'I should be watching my weight really but I can never resist this.' She popped another forkful into her mouth and closed her eyes in bliss.

'So who else lives in the building?' asked Adele after a moment.

'Well, there are only us two on this floor but there are two larger flats down on the first floor. Toby has one of those—you know, Dr Nash. You met him, didn't you?'

'Yes, I did. He seemed very nice.'

'He is—a bit serious, but nice.'

'And the other flat?' Even as she asked Adele had a premonition and instinctively knew what Penny was about to say.

'Casey is living in that at the moment while he's house-hunting,' she said.

So, not only was she going to have to work with him, Adele thought wryly, it seemed she was going to have to live alongside him as well. She looked up and realised that a flush had touched Penny's cheeks.

'Actually,' said Penny, leaning forward slightly in a conspiratorial manner, 'he and I are a bit of an item at the moment.'

'Really?' Adele was surprised. She would never in a million years have put them together. 'Well, that's nice,' she heard herself say.

'It's only very early days yet.' Penny took a mouthful of wine. 'But I'm hopeful. And, you have to admit, he is gorgeous.' When Adele didn't reply she went on, 'How about you?'

'Me? How do you mean?' Adele frowned. For one moment she thought Penny wanted her to agree with her last remark and she wasn't at all sure she could do that.

'Yes, is there anyone special in your life?'

Adele took a deep breath. Why did it still hurt so much?

'No,' she said at last, 'no, there's no one special in my life at the moment.'

They chatted on for a while, mainly about Stourborne Abbas and the practice, then with a reluctant sigh Penny hauled herself to her feet. 'I must be going,' she said. 'I have some notes to sort out before I finish. I'll see you in the morning,' she added as Adele also scrambled to her feet.

'Yes.' She nodded. 'At eight-thirty sharp.' Seeing Penny's rather curious look, she explained, 'I've already been told that Dr Casey doesn't like to be kept waiting.'

'That's true,' Penny agreed, then as she reached the door she looked over her shoulder. 'He doesn't like that either,' she added.

'What?' Adele frowned.

'Being called "Doctor". He prefers plain Casey.'

'He said that,' said Adele slowly, 'but I wasn't sure he meant it.'

'Oh, he meant it all right,' said Penny with a laugh. 'In fact, you can be sure that anything Casey says he means.'

After Penny had gone Adele was about to take herself off to the local supermarket to stock up on some food but, on opening the fridge to store the remains of the wine, she discovered fresh bread, milk, butter and cheese and decided that any shopping expedition could wait until the following day. No doubt Penny had been the one who had stocked her fridge and her thoughtfulness, together with the warmth of her welcome, did much to raise Adele's flagging spirits. It was, however, with a certain amount of apprehension that she anticipated her first day in the practice because nothing was to be as she had imagined and she had the feeling that life with Casey was going to be vastly different from life with Edward.

CHAPTER TWO

CASEY looked different next morning. The leathers had gone, replaced by a sweater and cords. It was still a far cry from a conventional suit and tie, but Adele had the feeling there was very little about this man that was conventional.

'Good morning.' That level gaze met hers as she paused in the open doorway of his consulting room at two minutes before eight-thirty. 'I trust you slept well.'

'Like a log, thank you.'

'Come in.' He indicated a chair. 'I've been working out a schedule for us. To start with, I want you to familiarise yourself thoroughly with the practice and the way it's run. That means, of course, getting to know the staff and studying the administration side of things and the system for clinics and surgeries. As you know, I wasn't around when you came for your interview so you'll have to enlighten me—did you meet all the other members of staff?'

'I think so.' Adele sat down. 'That's not to say I can remember all their names. There seem to be quite a lot of them.'

'There are,' he agreed. 'Let's recap—the partners include Edward and myself, of course, and Jeanette Maynard and Toby Nash. You did meet Jeanette and Toby?'

'Yes, I did.' Adele nodded. 'They were both very welcoming and seemed to like the idea of a trainee joining the practice. I hope I will be able to contribute something to the practice as well as benefiting from completing my training.' She wasn't sure what had prompted her to say

20

that—probably it was a throwback to the previous day's slightly abrasive first meeting with this man who had seemingly found himself in the unexpected and unwanted position of being her trainer.

'I would think your measure of contribution will be stretched to the limits,' he remarked dryly. 'This is a very busy practice,' he added, 'just in case you weren't aware. We are the only practice in Stourborne Abbas and we serve a large area around the town, including several outlying villages and hamlets.'

'Edward told me that you are also the local police surgeon for the area.'

'That's correct.' He nodded and Adele couldn't help but notice that the scar on his face seemed to stand out even more that morning, prompting her to wonder anew how he had come by it.

'That sort of work interests me,' she said, 'and I was wondering if I could accompany you sometimes?'

'When I'm called out on a case, you mean?' He spoke in a somewhat dramatic fashion, raising his eyebrows, and for a fraction of a second she had the feeling that he was patronising her.

'Yes, not that I imagine you have anything too sensational happening in Stourborne Abbas,' she said coolly.

'You'd be surprised,' he replied. 'This may look like a sleepy little backwater to the casual observer but it has more than its fair share of happenings. But, yes, certainly you can come if it doesn't affect your work here too much—I'll bear it in mind.'

'Maybe I could come with you if you get called out of surgery hours,' said Adele.

'Quite.' He leaned back in his chair and linked his hands behind his head. 'Now, what I propose is that you spend a period of time sitting in on my surgeries—after that we'll do a role reversal and I'll sit in while you take some surgeries.'

'And after that?'

'You'll take your own surgeries. We have more than enough extra patients every day to make up the numbers for an additional surgery. During that time I suggest you report to me, first on a daily basis and then, as you become more accustomed to the work, maybe weekly, unless, of course, you encounter any problems or difficulties, in which case I would expect you to come to me immediately.' He paused and stared intently at her. 'Does that sound reasonable to you?'

'Yes.' Adele nodded. 'But there is one thing I should like to know.'

'And what's that?' His eyes narrowed slightly.

'Somehow I've gained the impression that you were less than happy with the decision to take on a trainee. Am I right?'

He didn't answer immediately and Adele came to the conclusion that he had been taken unawares by her question and that he was considering his answer carefully.

'I was on sabbatical when the arrangements were made,' he said slowly at last.

'But surely your opinion was sought before you went— it is, after all, I would have thought, quite an important issue.'

'It was Edward in the first place who was keen to take on a trainee and he persuaded Jeanette and Toby of the supposed benefits for the practice. As you know, circumstances have changed since then and it was me as Edward's GP who had to point out to him that it was out of the question for him to even think of taking on the responsibilities of a trainee.'

'But before then,' Adele persisted, 'did Edward convince you of the benefits?'

'Let's just say that over this issue I was outnumbered.'

'So if you were the only one who wasn't happy with the situation, wouldn't it have made more sense for one of the other partners to take over as trainer when the circumstances changed?'

'It wasn't practical,' he replied calmly. 'Jeanette has personal problems at the present time and is unable to take on any extra duties and Toby is only a junior partner himself—so as it was unanimously felt that we shouldn't let you down, it was down to me.'

'I'm not sure that I'm happy with that,' said Adele quietly.

'I'm sorry?' Removing his hands from behind his head, Casey sat forward in his chair and stared at her in apparent amazement.

'I said I'm not sure that I'm happy having as my trainer someone who would rather I wasn't here.'

'I didn't say I would rather you weren't here…all I'm saying is that I alone amongst the partners wasn't in favour of having a trainee.'

'Doesn't that amount to the same thing?'

'Not at all. My reason for not wanting a trainee has nothing to do with you personally. I simply didn't feel the practice would benefit from a trainee at this particular time.'

'So you don't think there's enough here for me to do, is that it?'

'No,' he replied crisply, 'there's more than enough—too much, in fact.'

'Then I don't understand…' Adele looked bewildered.

'I said I didn't want a trainee at this time,' he said patiently, 'because I happen to think the practice is in desperate need of another fully trained partner.'

'Oh,' she said. 'Oh, I see…' Suddenly she felt quite deflated again.

'Does that answer your question?'

'Yes…'

'There will be more than enough here for you to do—you mark my words, you'll soon be begging for time off,' he added with a hint of a smile.

'It can't be any worse than the hours I was doing at the hospital…'

'We shall see,' he replied briskly. 'Now, I was telling you about the staff—apart from the partners, we have two full-time practice nurses, Penny Rudge and Fatima Oram, and there are two part-time nurses who cover for them. Our practice manager, as you know, is Rachel Tait. We have four reception staff and our secretary, Frances Drew, who seems to have been here longer than anyone. If there's anything you want to know you only have to ask Frances.' He broke off as there came a knock at the door. 'Come in,' he called.

The door opened and a young woman with red hair and a creamy complexion entered the room. She threw a startled glance at Adele as if she hadn't expected her to be there. 'I'm sorry, Casey,' she said, 'I didn't think you had anyone with you.'

'It's all right, Lizzie.' He indicated Adele and introduced her. 'This is Dr Brooks. Adele, this is Lizzie Vale, one of our receptionists.'

'Oh, I'm sorry, Dr Brooks.' The girl smiled and held out her hand. 'Welcome to Woolverton House.'

'Thank you, Lizzie, and, please, call me Adele.' They shook hands.

'Was there a problem, Lizzie?' Casey asked.

'Afraid so. Mrs Procter phoned and asked for an emergency visit. Mary spoke to her and she's now agreed to settle for an ordinary house call but only on condition that she speaks to you first.'

'When does she want to speak to me?'

'Now?' asked Lizzie fearfully, pulling a face as she spoke.

'She's still on the line?' Casey looked at the telephone on his desk.

''Fraid so.' Lizzie nodded. 'There really isn't any budging her and she's blocking the line, which is pretty desperate at this time of the morning.'

'OK, Lizzie, I'll sort it. Are those my notes?' He nodded at the bundle of patient records that Lizzie was carrying.

'Oh, yes.' She passed them across the desk then looked at Adele. 'Are you sitting in on Casey's surgery this morning?'

'Am I?' Adele glanced at Casey.

'Why not?' He glanced through the records. 'It'll be a baptism of fire, judging by this lot, but it'll be good for you. Perhaps you'd tell the patients that we have a trainee sitting in this morning, Lizzie. But, please, make sure you explain that Adele has already qualified as a doctor and that she most definitely is not a student.'

'Of course.' Lizzie grinned and left the room, and with a barely audible sigh Casey picked up the receiver. 'Flo?' he said. 'It's Casey here. Now, what's all this fuss about this morning?' He listened patiently for several minutes then he said, 'Right, give him some painkillers and tell him to lie flat. OK, if he can't get up the stairs tell him to lie on the floor. Tell Maudie I'll listen to her chest when I come in and if I think it's necessary I'll prescribe another course of antibiotics—and tell her if I find she's been smoking again I'll skin her alive. And I'll have a look at

Stevie at the same time—stomach upset you say. Was he
out last night? Probably too much lager. But I'll be over
later. Bye, Flo.' He hung up and turned to Adele.

'Flo is quite a character,' he said when he caught sight
of her expression, which in spite of herself was one of
amazement. 'She's been married three times, divorced
once, widowed once and wishes she'd never set eyes on
number three, let alone married him. She has eight children, most of whom still live in or around the family home,
and her elderly mother, Maudie, also lives there. There's
a crisis of some description probably every week. So, are
you ready to face the fray?' He reached out his hand to
press the buzzer for the first patient.

'Why did you say that to Lizzie about telling the patients
that I'm not a student?' asked Adele curiously as they
waited for the first patient.

'There is often a curious reaction to a student sitting in
and listening to their problems,' he replied. 'They question
it and they aren't always too happy about it.'

'And a trainee?'

'Oh, they like that. As soon as they know they have the
attention of two doctors…'

'Two for the price of one, you mean?'

'Something like that.' They were still smiling when the
first patient knocked on the door and came into the room.
Somehow the episode with Flo and her family problems
had lightened the atmosphere between them and by the
time the patient had sat down and told them all about the
pain he was getting from his bunions, Adele found she
was feeling less as if she was a nuisance who was simply
getting in the way and more like someone who might actually be an asset to the practice.

If Casey's term of 'baptism of fire' was something of
an exaggeration, the morning's list nevertheless presented

Adele with an insight into the diversity that an ordinary morning surgery could bring—a young mum with a fractious, teething baby closely followed the patient with the bunions, then a teenager with a tongue piercing that had gone septic preceded an anxious young man whose face was ravaged by acne. They'd barely drawn breath when a middle-aged woman having menopausal problems confronted them, followed by a man who had been bleeding heavily from the rectum and who required an urgent referral for further tests.

At the start of the surgery after the call from Flo Procter, Adele had had decided reservations about Casey's approach to his patients, believing that it was too casual, but as the morning wore on and she witnessed at first hand the response of the patients to his manner she was forced to revise her opinions.

As the surgery ended, Rachel Tait, the practice manager, phoned through to ask Casey and Adele to join the rest of the staff for coffee in the staffroom.

'I think this is by way of a welcome to you,' said Casey as he replaced the receiver. 'And an opportunity for you to meet the staff all together.' He paused. 'Tell me, did you find that list too daunting?'

'My "baptism of fire"?' Adele raised her eyebrows and smiled. 'Not at all. In actual fact, I enjoyed it.'

'Ah, the enthusiasm of the young and uninitiated...' That rare smile touched his rugged features as he stood up and opened the door for her to precede him out of the room.

It was true Adele had enjoyed her morning and she was feeling a lot better about the whole situation than she had the previous evening, in spite of the fact that Casey had admitted that he'd been so against having a trainee in the practice.

The staffroom at the side of Woolverton House was large and overlooked the garden. Adele had not yet had the opportunity of exploring the garden and as through the windows she caught a glimpse of copper beech and a large blue cedar on the lawn she promised herself that was a treat to come. The room was full of people, some she recognised and others she'd never seen before. Rachel came to meet them as they moved into the centre of the room.

'Adele, it's good to see you again,' Rachel said warmly. 'I looked for you this morning but I was told that this slave-driver…' she glanced up at Casey with a grin '…had your nose to the grindstone at eight-thirty sharp.'

'That's true,' Casey agreed. 'No time like the present for these things, in my opinion.'

'Yes, well, I think there's a time and a place for everything,' said Rachel firmly, 'and now is the time to welcome Adele properly to Woolverton House.'

'Hear! Hear!' Suddenly Edward was beside them and must have heard Rachel's comment. 'Adele.' He beamed. 'Did you survive your first surgery?'

'Well, I didn't really have to do anything.' Adele gave a little shrug. 'I just listened.'

'Sometimes that can be pretty daunting in itself,' Edward observed shrewdly. 'Now, let me see,' he went on, looking around the big room, 'whom haven't you met?'

The next half-hour was taken up with Adele meeting those staff members she hadn't met at her interview and renewing acquaintance with those she had. One of these was the practice's female partner. Jeanette Maynard was an attractive woman in her mid-forties and Adele already knew she was a divorcee with a teenage son and daughter.

'We're so pleased to have you aboard,' she told Adele as they spent a few moments together. 'Me, especially. I get hopelessly outnumbered against the men sometimes, it'll be nice to have another woman's point of view at partners' meetings.'

'Do you think they'll listen to what a humble trainee has to say?' asked Adele with a smile.

'Don't worry, I'll make sure they do,' replied Jeanette firmly. 'Now, tell me, are you quite comfortable in the flat?'

'Oh, yes.' Adele nodded. 'I slept very well last night. Mind you, I was dog-tired.'

'But you have everything you need?'

'Oh, yes.' She paused. 'There was even food in the fridge, bread and milk and things like that. I'm not sure who I have to thank for that.'

'I'm afraid it wasn't me,' said Jeanette with a laugh. 'Although I wish I had thought of it.'

'It was probably Penny,' said Adele. 'She came in to welcome me when I arrived. I must thank her later—it certainly saved me having to think about shopping last night.' Looking round, Adele caught sight of Penny. She was standing in the large window bay and was in conversation with Casey, her eyes shining and her expression animated, and just for a moment Adele was reminded that Penny had told her that the two of them were at the start of a relationship. The memory came with a jolt probably because even when she had first heard it, it had seemed improbable, and now that she knew Casey a little better it seemed even more so.

'Hello, Adele.'

She was brought swiftly back to the proceedings by a voice at her elbow. Turning sharply, she realised that Jeanette had turned away and was talking to Frances Drew, the practice secretary, and that it was Toby Nash, the junior partner, who had spoken to her.

'Hello, Toby,' she said, and found that she was relieved

that something had diverted her attention away from the unlikely couple in the window. She couldn't have explained why she was relieved, she only knew she was.

'Sorry, I haven't had a chance to speak to you yet.' Toby's eyes were serious behind his glasses while his mop of black hair flopped over his forehead.

'That's all right. I'm sure there will be plenty of opportunity later,' said Adele. 'After all, I believe we're neighbours as well as colleagues.' As she spoke she was amused to see that Toby's face had grown quite pink at the prospect of deepening their acquaintance.

'Don't you let Casey work you too hard,' he muttered to cover his embarrassment.

'I understand he's something of a slave-driver,' Adele commented wryly.

'He's a workaholic,' said Toby. 'Eats and sleeps work and seems to live solely for his patients.'

'Which I'm sure is very commendable, although maybe tough for others in his life to live with.'

'Oh, he's not married,' said Toby quickly.

'I was meaning more his colleagues,' Adele replied.

'Oh, yes, I see what you mean...' Toby trailed off as Edward suddenly called for quiet and all heads turned to where he was standing in front of the vast fireplace.

'You all know why you're here,' he said, looking round at his partners and the members of his staff, 'and that is to welcome Adele Brooks into the practice. Adele, as you know, is to do her GP training year with us here at Woolverton House. She comes to us from Chester where she did her medical training.' He stopped, looked round again then cleared his throat. 'As I'm sure you are all aware,' he went on after a moment, 'it was originally intended that I was to be Adele's trainer but unfortunately recent events have decreed otherwise. I am indebted to

Casey who has stepped into the breech and who will take over as Adele's trainer.' He paused and looked over his glasses at Casey who inclined his head slightly in response. 'For the rest of you,' Edward continued, 'I would like you to make every effort to give Casey any help you can and, of course, to assist Adele in every possible way. She is new to the area and knows neither the patients nor you, the members of staff. This, I know from experience, can be a daunting situation. Please, all of you, be aware of it and do all you can to make Adele's year amongst us a happy and pleasant one during which she will learn what is necessary to take forward into her life as a GP.'

It was obvious that he had finished and Adele was aware that all eyes had turned to her, compelling her to think that she should say something in response.

Nervously she cleared her throat then, breaking the silence, she said, 'Thank you, Edward, for that kind welcome. I'm sure from what I've seen so far that I'm going to be very happy here at Woolverton House. I would also like to thank Casey for agreeing to take over my training at such short notice and the rest of you for your kind welcome on my arrival—for the flowers and the wine and for whoever prepared the flat so thoughtfully.' She stopped and for a fraction of a second her gaze caught Casey's and for the second time she saw on his face that expression that she'd been unable to define. It had been there the previous day when they had first met and it was there again now as he stood at the window, watching her. It unnerved her slightly and she stumbled over what she intended saying next.

'I…would like…' She trailed off then took a deep breath and started again. 'What Edward said is very true. I am unused to this way of life so I hope you will all help me to find my feet. I am, however, no stranger to hard work so if there's anything you think I may be able to help with, don't be afraid to ask.'

After coffee and biscuits, which were served by Lizzie Vale and another receptionist, Cheryl Burgess, the gathering gradually dispersed and everyone returned to work.

As Adele prepared to leave the room Rachel joined her. 'Adele,' she said, 'would you like to come along to the office? There are a few things I need to go through with you, like tax and insurance details and your terms of contract.'

'All right.' Adele nodded then found herself looking over her shoulder. 'I'd better just tell Casey,' she said.

While Rachel went on Adele waited until Casey and Penny came out of the big room. Penny was still chattering non-stop but for the briefest of moments Adele got the impression that Casey wasn't listening to her, and as they approached it was her he was looking at.

'Were you waiting for me?' he asked and Penny stopped in mid-sentence.

'Only to say that Rachel has asked me to go to the office to sort out my details,' Adele replied.

'Fair enough.' Casey nodded. 'After that we have a house call to make.'

'You want me to come with you?'

'Absolutely. Or maybe my description of the Procter household put you off visiting them?' There was a touch of sarcasm in his voice and Penny grinned.

'No, of course not,' said Adele quickly. 'I'll come to your room when Rachel has finished with me.'

It didn't take too long to go through her personal details and when they had finished, Rachel said, 'Are you getting on all right with Casey?'

'Yes, I think so.' Adele nodded slowly. 'I wasn't quite

sure how to take him at first,' she admitted, 'but I think we'll be OK.'

'He certainly isn't quite like your average GP, is he?' Rachel smiled. 'I always say he missed his vocation and that he should have pursued some sort of action career like the SAS or a stunt man. But, having said that, he's a good doctor so maybe he was right after all. Certainly his patients think the world of him.'

'One thing does intrigue me about him,' said Adele.

'Only one?' Rachel raised an eyebrow then with a chuckle she said, 'What's that?'

'Why does everyone call him Casey?'

'It's his name,' said Rachel with a shrug.

'Yes, I know, but doesn't he have a first name?'

'He does but he hates it. Only Edward and myself know what it is for legal and administrative purposes and we are sworn to secrecy on pain of death. All he will admit to is the initial H which he uses when forced to sign official documents.'

'Oh,' said Adele. 'I see.' The explanation was fair enough but somehow it just seemed to add yet another dimension to the unconventional aura that surrounded the man who was her trainer.

CHAPTER THREE

'WE'D better take the Land Rover,' Casey said, glancing at Adele's short, straight skirt as they walked out of the building into the rear courtyard.

'I don't mind going on the bike if you'd rather,' she offered.

By this time he had unlocked the Land Rover and was behind the wheel. He seemed to hesitate for a moment then he said, 'No, we'll take this.'

She climbed up beside him, remaining silent as he reversed out of the space then inched out of the courtyard to attempt to join the traffic in the high street. It was as busy as ever with constant streams of cars and delivery vehicles and dozens of shoppers milling across the pavements.

'Is it always like this?' she asked, throwing him a sidelong glance.

'Pretty much.' He pulled a face then gave a thumbs-up sign as a tradesman's van gave way, allowing him out of the mews entrance. 'It's one of the reasons I use the bike so often.'

'Maybe in future I'd better change into trousers for house calls.'

'You can wear trousers for surgery as far as I'm concerned.'

She opened her mouth to say that she considered a skirt and jacket more suitable for surgery but then shut it again. How could she talk about such things to this man who himself was so unconventional in his ways? No doubt in the height of summer he would think nothing of conducting surgery wearing shorts and a T-shirt.

They drove in silence through the heavy traffic then as they sat at a set of traffic lights, waiting for the green light, he half turned towards her. 'Everything go all right with Rachel?' he asked.

'Yes.' Adele nodded. 'It was only a chat to sort out tax codes and the terms of my contract.'

'And are you happy with the terms of your contract?'

'Oh, yes. Yes, I think so.' It hadn't occurred to her to question it. Now she wondered if maybe she should have done but at the time everything had seemed more than reasonable with regard to her working hours, time off and holidays.

'Rachel's OK,' he said. 'She'll sort out any admin problems you might have—she's even been known to sort out other sorts of problems,' he added dryly.

'Other sorts of problems?' Adele threw him a startled glance. 'What do you mean?'

'Personal problems—you know, relationship problems, the sort of problems that inevitably arise after boy meets girl.'

'Oh,' said Adele. 'I see.'

'And as I'm sure you can imagine, we have plenty of those with a high proportion of young women on the staff.'

'Are you saying that men don't experience such problems?' she raised her eyebrows.

'Not at all. I'm sure they do. The difference is that they choose not to talk about them.'

'So Rachel is good at helping to sort these things out?'

'I understand she's a good listener, that together with the fact that she has the patience of a saint.' He gave a short laugh. 'We had an episode recently where both Lizzie and Cheryl had boyfriend trouble—they were commiserating with each other until they discovered it was over the same man. After that there was so much flak about you needed a hard hat just to go into Reception.'

Adele laughed. 'They seem friendly enough now.'

'Oh, yes, the boyfriend was sent packing. They've both moved on and I imagine there are new men on the scene—hopefully, this time they will have one each.' He paused and threw Adele a sidelong glance. 'What about you, Dr Brooks?' he asked.

'What about me?' asked Adele.

'Do you have boyfriend trouble?'

'Oh, no, nothing like that, I can assure you.'

There was a long pause. 'Do you mean you don't have trouble with your boyfriend,' he asked at last, 'or that you don't have trouble because you don't have a boyfriend?'

'I don't have trouble because I don't have a boyfriend.' Adele bit her lip. Why did even thinking of it cause a wave of misery to wash over her? She should be over it now after all this time.

'I find that very hard to believe.' He had taken his eyes from the road, albeit briefly, to stare at her in apparent amazement.

'I don't see why,' she retorted.

'I would have thought they would have been beating a path to your door—hordes of them,' he added.

'Hardly.' She gave a little snort of derision. Turning her head, she gazed out of the window. They were travelling out of the town now into a heavily populated residential area.

'So are you saying there's no one?' He was nothing if not persistent and, irritated, she turned back.

'No, there isn't—not now.' She wasn't sure why she added the rider and immediately wished she hadn't. He, of course, seized upon it.

'So there was someone, is that it?'

What was the point in denying it? Talking of it might be painful but it was no secret. 'Yes, there was someone,' she admitted.

'Recently?'

'Until six months ago.'

'Husband? Live-in lover? Boyfriend?' His gaze was straight now as they negotiated several bends in the road and began climbing a hill.

'You want to know an awful lot,' she protested.

He shrugged. 'If we're to work closely together I think it's important we know where we're coming from, and that includes understanding past history.'

'OK.' She took a deep breath, bracing herself. 'He was a live-in lover. We didn't get as far as marriage or even an engagement, although I believed it was heading in that direction.'

'What went wrong?' There was a softer note in his voice now.

Adele hesitated, unsure how much she should be revealing, then it was her turn to shrug. What the hell did it matter? Casey didn't know Nigel and they were never likely to meet. It was all history now, painful history, but history none the less. 'He went home to visit his family one weekend,' she said at last. 'I had to work, but after he'd gone I found I could get away after all so I decided to surprise him by joining him and his family.'

'What happened? Did you get more than you'd bargained for?'

'You could say that.' She pulled a face. 'I knew they were well off, what I hadn't realised was just how well off. We're talking serious money here—a country estate, a London town-house, that sort of thing. The whole thing was a nightmare. It soon became obvious that his family had never even heard of me. His mother was a frightful snob who looked down her nose at me and made it perfectly plain that her son's affections lay elsewhere.'

'And did they?' asked Casey curiously.

'Yes, I think they did. There was a young woman there from another terribly rich family who seemed to think that she and Nigel—that was his name—had some long-standing arrangement.'

'I take it you tackled him about this?' Casey half turned towards her, raising one eyebrow, the gesture while questioning also indicating disgust at what he was hearing.

'Of course,' she retorted.

'And did they—have some long-standing arrangement?'

'Yes, it appears they did. The idea was that they would marry eventually, so merging the two families' wealth.'

'So what was your part in all this?'

'To start with I suppose I was just a diversion—a bit on the side if you like,' she added bitterly. 'Later it got rather more serious and Nigel confessed he hadn't known how to tell me about Lucinda Ratsey-Pemberton.'

'Good grief, was that her name?' Casey looked startled. 'What happened? What did you do?'

'Ended it immediately.' Adele tilted her chin. 'Chucked him out of my flat and got on with my life.'

'Good for you.' Casey brought the Land Rover to a halt and switched off the engine. They sat for a while in silence while Adele stared out of the windscreen with unseeing eyes as she tried desperately to quell the tide of feelings surging inside her as she relived those final days with Nigel.

'Trouble is,' said Casey at last, breaking the silence between them, 'it's never that easy, is it?'

'What?' Wildly she turned her head to look at him. He was staring thoughtfully at her through narrowed eyes.

'The end of a long-term relationship. It hurts, whatever the circumstances, and in your case it must have been doubly so because you had been deceived as well.'

'Yes,' she gulped. 'It did hurt—still does, if I'm honest. But I'm getting there.'

'Good for you.' Casey said, then he glanced out of the window. 'After all that do you feel ready to face the Procter brood?'

'After that I think I could face anything,' she said shakily. Surprisingly she found she meant it. She'd hardly talked to anyone about Nigel and why they had parted, but by telling Casey, who hadn't been in any way involved, she seemed to have released something, whether anger or pain she wasn't quite sure. Whatever it was, it had a cathartic effect and made her feel marginally better.

As Casey began to climb out of the vehicle she found herself looking at their surroundings. While they'd been driving she'd become so caught up in her emotions that she hadn't taken any notice of the area but now she realised that they seemed to be in the centre of a vast housing estate. Rows and rows of identical houses stretched for as far as the eye could see while the skyline was only relieved by a few blocks of bleak, high-rise flats. They had parked in front of what had obviously once been a little shopping mall but which now housed only a take-away and a betting shop, the rest of the units being boarded up.

A group of youths lolled against the railings of the mall, eyeing the Land Rover as Casey and Adele climbed out. Casey turned and looked at them. 'Don't even think about it,' he said warningly.

'All right, then, Casey?' called one of the youths.

Adele looked quickly at Casey to see his reaction to such familiarity but he merely nodded.

'Who's your bird?' said another.

'She isn't my bird. This is Dr Brooks.' Casey placed great emphasis on the word 'doctor'. 'You'll be seeing her around for the next year or so.'

'Phwoar!' The response was collective.

'She can feel my bits any time she likes...'

'I think I'm dying, Dr Brooks...'

'Doctor, come and have a look at this...'

Adele was aware of only two things—the fact that her cheeks had flushed and the smile on Casey's face as they crossed the road and approached one of the houses.

'You'll get used to it,' he said. 'They're a rough bunch but the answer is to give as good as you get.'

'What happens if the Land Rover is minus its wheels when we come out?' she remarked dryly.

'I'd have them—and they know it,' he replied grimly. 'Now, let's see what delights the Procters have for us to-day. As you will have noticed, the houses are all the same—three-bedroomed semi-detached. The Procters only differ in that they have two houses knocked into one to accommodate them all.'

The garden resembled a scrap merchant's yard, with the burnt-out shell of an old car and the parts of at least two motorbikes strewn around. There were skateboards, children's scooters, a vast selection of plastic toys, a rusty barbeque, an old television set, a fridge minus its door and two wheelie-bins stuffed to overflowing with rubbish and kitchen waste. A thin, biscuit-coloured mongrel was tied to the broken stumps of what had once been a fence and on the doorstep two small children were playing with a bowl of soapy water and some empty jars. One of them looked up as Casey and Adele approached.

'Hello,' said Casey. 'It's Robbie, isn't it?'

'No,' said the child, 'I'm Ronan.'

'And I'm Madonna,' said the little girl solemnly, looking up at them through a tangle of blonde hair.

'Madonna…?' murmured Adele.

'I should have warned you,' Casey began, then stopped as Ronan suddenly lifted his head and yelled at the top of his lungs.

'Mam! Casey's 'ere!'

A moment later Flo Procter's awesome presence filled the doorway, a woman of vast proportions. Adele found herself wondering whether child number nine might be on the way then decided that it was too difficult to tell.

'Casey.' Flo, nodding curtly, addressed Casey but at the same time eyed Adele speculatively. ''Bout time, we'd almost given you up. Who's this?' she added. She made no attempt to move aside.

'This is Dr Brooks,' Casey explained. 'She's with us for a year while she completes her GP training.'

'Student, then,' said Flo.

'No, not a student, Flo. Adele is a fully qualified doctor. She just needs to gain experience of what it takes to deal with the demands of being a GP.'

'Dealing with the likes of us, you mean?' Flo chuckled suddenly and unexpectedly.

'Something like that, Flo,' Casey agreed. 'Now, are you going to let us in?'

Flo moved aside into the doorway of what was obviously a living room and Adele followed Casey into the hall, which was crammed with coats, bikes, empty bottles and wellington boots.

'He's in here,' said Flo, then as first Adele, then Casey, squeezed past her into the living room she stared intently at Adele. 'You got Irish blood in you, love?'

'Yes, as it happens.' Adele nodded and smiled. 'My grandmother was Irish.'

'I knew it.' Flo grinned with satisfaction. 'Well, there he is,' she added darkly.

The living room was chaotic, with part of a fish and chip meal still in its paper wrapping on the wooden table, which was also littered with what looked like the remains of the previous evening's meal. A huge television set blared out in one corner of the room and piles of old newspapers and magazines covered every surface.

A man was lying on the threadbare carpet, watching the television, his head supported by a couple of thick cushions. He looked up, startled, as Flo picked up the remote control and muted the sound. Catching sight of Casey and Adele, he immediately adopted an expression of intense suffering.

'Hello, Mick,' Casey crouched beside him. 'What's the problem?'

'It's me back again, Casey,' whined Mick Procter. 'It's gone. All I did was bend over and I heard it go. Can't move, I can't.'

'Right, Mick, let's have a look at you.' Adele watched as Casey proceeded to examine Mick. It was no easy matter as it soon became evident that the man was genuinely in a fair amount of pain and found it difficult to move.

'Well,' said Casey at last as he completed his examination by testing the man's reflexes, 'you know the drill. This isn't the first time this disc has played up. You lie flat, so first of all let's get rid of those cushions.' As he spoke he eased the cushions from under Mick's neck 'I'll prescribe some painkillers and a muscle relaxant. I think it's probably also time we organised another X-ray then we'll see about some physiotherapy.'

'Oh, no,' groaned Mick, 'not that again.'

Ignoring him, Casey began scribbling out a prescription.

'So where you living, love?' Flo, seemingly oblivious to her husband's predicament, turned to Adele.

'In one of the flats at Woolverton House,' Adele replied only after a hesitant glance at Casey. She wasn't quite certain how much information she should divulge.

'Oh, yes.' Flo looked interested. 'I knew someone who had one of those flats. Elvira Jackson—is she still there?'

It was Casey who answered, tearing off the prescription and handing it to Flo. 'No,' he said, 'Elvira has moved on.'

'Strange one, that, and no mistake.' Flo folded the prescription and tucked it into her blouse. 'You said you'd take a look at Mum while you're here, Casey—she's in the other room.' Leaving the hapless Mick on the floor, minus his cushions and unable to reach the remote control, they all trooped through the house to a smaller room at the rear where an elderly woman sat in a corner, watching yet another television and wheezing noisily with every breath she took.

'Hello, Maudie,' said Casey cheerfully. 'How are we today?'

'Well, I don't know how you are,' rasped the old woman, 'but I feel blooming awful.'

'In that case we'd better see what we can do about it. Let's have a listen to that chest.' Casey took the stethoscope from his bag then passed it to Adele.

'Me?' she said, startled.

'Why not? You've got to start somewhere,' Casey replied, his gaze meeting hers.

Maudie looked up in sudden alarm. 'Here, wait a minute,' she snapped. 'I'm not having no one practising on me.'

'She's not practising, Mum,' said Flo. 'She's a doctor

same as Casey—she's come to help them out up at Woolverton House.'

'But he said she had to start somewhere.' Maudie was obviously still very suspicious and clutched at the front of her blouse with bony fingers. 'She ain't starting with me and that's it and all about it.'

'He meant she had to start getting to know people, didn't you, Casey?'

'That's exactly what I meant,' said Casey. 'Now, come on, Maudie, be reasonable or I'll start asking the kids how many cigarettes you've been smoking.'

The old lady began grumbling under her breath but at last, reluctantly, she opened her blouse and allowed Adele to listen first to her chest and then her back.

'Took your time, didn't you?' she muttered as Adele finished her examination and removed the stethoscope from her ears. 'Casey don't take that long.'

'Well?' Casey looked at Adele.

'There's congestion and base crackles,' Adele replied.

'Another course of antibiotics, Maudie.' Casey sat down on the arm of a chair took out his prescription pad for the second time since entering the Procter household. Balancing it on his knee, he began writing. 'Are you using your inhalers, Maudie?' he asked without looking up.

'Course I am,' she wheezed. 'I wouldn't get far without them.'

'Right.' Casey handed the prescription to Flo. 'Another one for you, Flo.'

'I'll get Elton to pick them up,' she said.

'When you phoned you said something about Stevie,' said Casey as he stood up. 'Where is he?'

'Don't know.' Flo shrugged. 'He went out. I told him to wait. I said you wouldn't like it.'

'So was he better?' Casey sounded annoyed and Adele

threw him a wary glance. Casey in a good mood was one thing; Casey in a bad mood, she suspected, would be something else entirely.

'Said he was,' Flo replied. 'You were probably right when you said it was too much lager last night. Mind you, he did have a terrible guts ache this morning. Rolling around he was. I tell you, what with him and Mick…' She didn't finish the sentence but it was pretty obvious that her sentiments towards her family were a little less than sympathetic.

A few moments later Adele found herself, together with Casey, on the pavement outside the Procters' house.

'Phew!' she said.

'What's up?' Casey raised one eyebrow but there was a glint of amusement in his eyes.

'Well, I have to say that was quite an experience. But tell me,' she said, as they made their way back to the Land Rover, 'do all the children have pop-star names?'

'Oh, yes,' Casey replied in a matter-of-fact tone. 'Flo lives in a world of pop stars—she always has done. I think they're her consolation against the reality of her life. The eldest boy is Elvis, by the way, but he's no longer at home.'

'Is he married?' asked Adele, bracing herself to run the gauntlet of the leering youths at the shopping mall. Their numbers seemed to have swelled alarmingly, which led her to wonder if someone had been despatched to round up others in order to gawp at the new doctor.

'No,' said Casey. 'He's in prison for nicking cars.'

There were a few jibes of a suggestive but reasonably good-natured fashion from the youths but Adele was relieved to see that the Land Rover appeared to be in one piece and within minutes they were heading back to Woolverton House.

Casey was silent to start with and then suddenly and totally unexpectedly he resumed their conversation of earlier. 'So, in view of recent events,' he said, 'can I assume that for the present you are off men in general?'

'Sorry?' Adele threw him a startled glance.

'Well, it would be perfectly understandable if you were. Trust takes a terrific bashing in such circumstances and trust is one of those things that's difficult to rebuild.'

'That's true,' she agreed slowly.

'So men are off your immediate agenda?'

'Well, yes, I suppose you could say that,' she admitted at last. She hadn't really thought about it, but now that he put it like that, she guessed it was true. The last thing she wanted was to rush headlong into another relationship after Nigel and, yes, she supposed trust could well be the factor that would prevent her from doing so. She'd thought she'd been able to trust Nigel and it had been a shock when she'd realised he'd been lying to her from the very beginning. Turning her head, she looked at the man at her side and once again she found herself feeling annoyed with him. This time it was because of the number of questions he'd asked her, all the things he seemed to want to know about her private life, and because he seemed to have had the uncanny knack of summing things up pretty accurately.

Thoroughly irritated, she heard herself say, 'So what about you?'

'What about me?' He was frowning now, a deep frown that was almost a scowl.

'Well, it was you who said if we were to work together you thought we should know each other's past history. I've told you mine...' She trailed off, waiting for him to continue.

'I'm also single,' he said after a long silence.

'I suppose you haven't found the right girl yet?' She

gave a short laugh but his sombre expression didn't change by so much as a flicker of an eyelid.

'It hasn't always been that way.'

'Really?' Suddenly she wasn't sure she wanted to know about the conquests in his life after all and was beginning to wish she hadn't asked.

'No,' he said quietly. 'I was married once.'

'Oh.' She stared at him. No one had said anything about an ex-wife.

'It was a long time ago. We were very young—I was still at medical school, actually.'

'I had friends who married while still doing their training. It put a tremendous strain on the marriage and it didn't last very long.'

'I was married for two years,' he said.

'If you don't mind me asking, why did you split up? Couldn't your wife put up with the long hours? Or was she training as well?'

'No, she was nurse.'

'So she should have known what your job entailed.'

'My wife didn't leave me,' he said, and there was an edge now to his voice that was difficult to identify.

'So you left her?'

'No,' he replied quietly. 'She died, giving birth to our baby.'

Adele stared at him in dismay, wishing the floor on her side of the Land Rover would open up and she could just disappear into a black hole. She had just assumed he was divorced, not widowed. How could she have been so insensitive?

'I'm so sorry,' she managed to say at last. 'I had no idea.'

'How could you have known?' He gave a slight shrug.

'It's not the sort of information I volunteer at a first meeting.'

'No, of course not, but I wish one of the others had told me and prevented me from putting my foot in it so terribly.'

'Like I say, it all happened a long time ago, long before I came to Stourborne Abbas. I don't suppose all the staff are even aware of it. Edward and Jeanette know, of course, and presumably Toby and Rachel, but I don't know about the others.'

She didn't know what else to say but in desperation felt she couldn't simply leave it there. 'But your child…the baby?'

'A little girl,' he replied, and his voice had softened again. 'She didn't stand a chance, she was just too premature—a little scrap of a thing. I had her baptised and she was buried with her mother.'

'That is just so sad.' Adele felt her eyes fill with tears. 'I really am very sorry, you know.'

'It's OK, really. You weren't to know.'

By this time they had reached Woolverton House and Casey drove into the courtyard. 'Lunchtime, I think,' he said, looking at his watch. 'I'll see you at two for afternoon surgery.'

'Yes, of course.' Adele nodded and made her way into the house, heading for the stairs, while Casey disappeared in the direction of his surgery. She was still reeling from all that he had told her. It somehow seemed inconceivable that he should have suffered so much tragedy.

It wasn't until later when she was eating her lunch that it occurred to her that while he had told her of his past life and his brief, tragic marriage he'd said nothing of the present and his relationship with Penny. If, as they'd agreed, they were coming clean over relationships, that seemed to her rather odd.

CHAPTER FOUR

ADELE met Casey promptly at two o'clock for afternoon surgery during which there proved to be every bit as much variety and diversity as there had been in morning surgery. When they finished Casey had house calls and when Adele asked if he wanted her to accompany him he shook his head. 'Not this time,' he said. 'I think you should spend some time in Reception, looking at the filing and appointment systems, and get one of the girls to show you the computer and the software that we use. I'll see you later.' With a wave of his hand he was gone, leaving a slightly bemused Adele standing at the reception desk.

'Are you all right, Adele?'

Adele turned and found Mary Kennington, the senior receptionist, peering at her over the desk.

'Yes, I think so. Dr…er…Casey has just said that I should spend some time getting to know how the system works.'

'Well, in that case you'd better come in here with us.' Mary opened the door beside the desk and Adele went into the office area that housed the patient records and the administration files. The other two receptionists, Cheryl and Lizzie, were working at computers and they both looked up as Adele came in.

'How's your first day going?' asked Cheryl.

'Casey not worked you to death yet?' said Lizzie with a grin.

'I've just finished the day's repeat prescriptions,' Mary explained. 'Maybe you'd like to start with seeing how we deal with them then we'll go on to the appointments system.'

Adele spent the next hour learning as much as she could about how the Woolverton House surgery worked. She was amazed at just how much there was to absorb and when she commented on it Mary suggested that she should come in each day for an hour or so until she was familiar with it all.

'Did you go to the Procters' with Casey?' asked Lizzie a little later as Adele was studying the staff rosters.

'I did indeed,' she replied.

'Nothing like chucking somebody in at the deep end,' remarked Cheryl with a laugh. 'What was wrong with Stevie, by the way?'

'I don't know.' Adele shook her head. 'He wasn't there. Apparently he'd made a miraculous recovery and gone out.'

'After all the fuss his mother made,' said Lizzie with a sigh. 'She made it sound like a matter of life and death on the phone. She was more concerned about him than poor old Mick, or Maudie come to that.'

'Maudie will use any excuse to see Casey,' said Mary. 'I think she's got a soft spot for him.'

'Maudie actually needed more antibiotics,' said Adele.

'Maudie always needs antibiotics,' chorused Mary, Cheryl and Lizzie.

'It's something to do with the number of cigarettes she smokes,' said Mary. 'So what did you think of the Bowscombe Estate?' she added.

'Well, it seemed a pretty tough area,' admitted Adele.

'That's putting it mildly.' Lizzie pulled a face. 'You wouldn't catch me walking through there after dark, I can tell you.'

'I'd think twice about walking there in daylight,' said Mary.

'Casey didn't seem to give it a second thought,' observed Adele. 'In fact, he seemed to know a lot of people there—would they all be registered here?'

'Well some of them are, but Casey probably knows the majority of them from wearing his other hat.'

'His other hat?' Adele frowned then it dawned on her what Mary meant. 'Oh, you mean as a police surgeon?'

'Exactly.' Mary nodded. 'A fair percentage of the population of the Bowscombe Estate spend half their time in police custody.' She paused, eyeing Adele speculatively. 'Are you going to be involved in that, Adele?'

'I hope so. It's an area of medicine that interests me a lot.'

'Rather you than me after hearing about some of the things Casey has to deal with down at the police station.' Cheryl gave a little shudder. At that moment the door opened and Penny came into Reception.

'All finished?' asked Mary.

'Yes, thank goodness.' Penny yawned and stretched then, catching sight of Adele, she said, 'What about you?'

It was Cheryl who answered on Adele's behalf. 'Well, she's survived her first day with Casey which involved a visit to the Bowscombe Estate *and* the Procters, so I say if she can survive that she'll survive anything.'

'Oh, absolutely,' said Penny with a laugh.

'Why don't you call it a day?' Mary turned to Adele. 'I would say you've had quite enough to contend with for your first day.'

'What about Casey?' asked Adele dubiously.

'What *about* Casey?' Mary raised her eyebrows.

'Well, I don't know if he wanted me to do anything

else,' Adele wrinkled her nose. 'He said "See you later" when he went out.'

'You leave Casey to me,' said Penny.

'Yes?' said Adele doubtfully.

'Absolutely,' said Penny firmly. 'You've done quite enough for one day. Besides, I'm sure there must be things you want to do.'

'As a matter of fact, I could do with doing a bit of shopping and getting the flat straight. Which reminds me, was it you, Penny, who stocked up the fridge?'

Penny shook her head, 'No, sorry. I can't lay claim to that. Maybe it was Rosie—she's a little gem like that.'

'Yes, maybe. I'll have to see her and thank her.'

Adele left Reception with her head buzzing with facts and figures. After collecting her jacket and bag, she left Woolverton House by the front entrance and stood for a moment on the steps, enjoying the warmth of the September afternoon. The supermarket was only a stone's throw from the surgery and it didn't take her long to load a trolley with food and other essentials. On her return there was no sign of Casey so, taking the advice of Penny and Mary, Adele made her way up to her flat. The next couple of hours she spent packing everything away and arranging the furniture and her possessions to her satisfaction, after which she lit several scented candles then began preparing the food she had bought for a meal.

While the food was cooking she took a long, leisurely soak in the bath where she found herself going over the events of the day. She was feeling quite exhausted, not from what she'd actually been doing but from all she had been expected to take in. Idly she wondered if Casey was back from his house calls and if he, too, was feeling tired. Somehow she doubted it, deciding it probably took a lot to weary him. She wondered if he and Penny were spending the evening together. Maybe Penny was cooking for him in her flat or perhaps he was doing the cooking if his flat was the more spacious of the two. She frowned as she tried to picture them together, finding it almost impossible. Round, bubbly-natured Penny with her non-stop chatter and Casey who was…well, what was Casey like? Adele found herself hard-pressed to sum him up and in the end gave up the attempt.

She wondered if they slept together and somehow found the idea almost as disturbing as learning about his wife. She'd been shocked and upset and terribly sad when he'd told her about the deaths of his wife and baby daughter but the thought of him sleeping with Penny disturbed her in another way, although she was unable to say why.

She was beginning to regret telling him so much about Nigel, even though in doing so she had felt a little better about the whole thing. What had happened between her and Nigel was private. Why, she hadn't even given the details to her friends or, with the exception of her sister Elaine, to her family, simply that they had decided to part. Somehow she'd doubted whether she could have coped with the utter humiliation if people had found out that Nigel had had someone else right from the beginning, and now she'd told a complete stranger all the gory details. Well, nearly all the details.

She hadn't told him about the terrible confrontation between herself and Nigel when she'd first realised that not only had Lucinda been there in the background of his life throughout the entire time they had been together, but that Lucinda had also been under the impression that they would shortly be married and that Nigel's parents had purchased a home for the happy couple in Cheshire.

Casey had observed that she would find it difficult to trust another man after such a betrayal and he was right.

Adele had found herself wondering in the time since she and Nigel had parted whether she would ever trust anyone again.

So lost had she become in her thoughts that it was with a little shock that when she moved she found that the bath water had grown cold. With a shiver she sat up, released the water then climbed out of the bath, wrapping a large fluffy bath sheet around her.

She ate a solitary meal then, on an impulse no doubt prompted by her reflections on the past, decided to phone her sister. She smiled to herself as she heard the phone ringing at the other end and pictured her sister flapping about in the permanent state of chaos in which she seemed to live. Elaine was four years older than Adele and married with three children. Their mother Jennifer constantly held Elaine up to Adele as an example of motherhood and a state to which she herself should be aspiring. 'But I'm a doctor, Mum,' Adele had protested on more than one occasion. 'It takes time and tremendous effort to become a doctor.'

'That shouldn't stop you from marrying and having children,' had been her mother's ready response. 'My GP is married and she has twin daughters.'

'She's probably a few years older than me,' Adele would reply wearily.

'Hello?'

'Hello, Lainey,' she said at the sound of her sister's voice. 'You sound harassed. Is this a bad time?'

'Is there ever a good time in this house?' Her sister sighed. 'Hi, Del, how are you? How's it going? Is it a nice place? What are the staff like? I've been thinking about you all day and wondering how you were getting on.'

'I'm fine. Exhausted, but fine. The house is beautiful but

I told you about that before, didn't I, after the interview? And so far the staff seem very nice.'

'What's your flat like?' demanded Elaine. 'You didn't see that before, did you?'

'No, it was still occupied then. But I have to say it's lovely. It's a big studio flat but has its own bathroom and kitchen so there's no sharing with anyone else, and the décor and furnishings are really very nice.' She looked around as she spoke, admiring the room suffused in the soft golden light from the lighted candles.

'And what about the staff?' Elaine obviously wanted to know everything. 'Have you made any friends?'

'Well, it's early days yet, of course, but they all seem OK. One girl in particular has gone out of her way to be friendly. Her name's Penny, Penny Rudge—she's one of the practice nurses and she also has one of the four flats above the practice.'

'And the other doctors, are they all right? What about your trainer—Dr Flemming, wasn't it?'

'No, you mean Dr Fletcher, Edward Fletcher—well, unfortunately there's been a bit of a hiccup there. He isn't able to be my trainer after all because he has heart trouble.'

'Well, that's a good start,' said Elaine. 'I hope they have someone else who can do it.'

'Oh, yes, they have someone else all right.'

'I didn't like the way you said that. Who is he and what's wrong with him?'

Adele sighed. She knew there was no hiding anything from Elaine. Her sister had always had the ability to read her like a book. 'His name is Casey—he's one of the partners here. I don't know that there's anything wrong with him exactly—he's just a bit different, that's all.'

'In what way different? You've got me curious now, Del.'

'Well, he's not a bit like Edward and, really, he's nothing like your average GP.'

'Well, go on. You can't leave it there. How's he different?'

'I suppose he comes across as a bit of a rough diamond. For a start he wears leathers and does his house calls on a motorbike.'

'Hmm, tell me more—he sounds intriguing.'

'I wouldn't call him intriguing exactly…'

'Is he good-looking?'

'Not really—sort of tough-looking, the type you wouldn't want to meet in a dark alley at night.'

'Or the type you might want to accompany you in a dark alley at night.' Elaine chuckled.

'Well, yes, I suppose so if you put it like that.'

'Is he spoken for?'

'I think so, at least Penny Rudge told me that he and she have just started a relationship…but…'

'But what?'

'I don't know. They just seem such an unlikely couple that's all. Penny's all lively and bubbly…and Casey, well… Anyway, it's none of my business. I guess I'll just have to get along with my new trainer as best I can. The one good thing—' her voice took on a brighter note '—is that Casey is also a police surgeon and he's said I can go with him sometimes when he's called out.'

'You always were interested in police work, weren't you?' said Elaine. Not waiting for a reply, she went on, 'Why do you call him Casey? Is that his first name?'

'No, his surname—but everyone uses it. No one knows what his first name is, only that it begins with the letter H.'

'It'll be Horace,' said Elaine. 'Remember Horace Barrington at school. He hated his name—we all called him Barry. Oh, by the way, while I'm thinking of it, I saw that rat Nigel the other day in town.'

Adele's heart lurched painfully. 'Did you?' she said in a small voice, wishing it didn't matter and at the same time hating herself that it still did.

'Yes,' said Elaine cheerfully. 'He looked as miserable as sin. Serves him right—he's probably found out that life with lovely Lucinda isn't what he'd thought.'

They talked on for a while and finished with Adele promising to ring their mother in the next couple of days and Elaine promising to ring Adele the next time. Once she'd hung up, tiredness seemed to get the better of her and she decided she may as well have an early night.

She was asleep almost as soon as she closed her eyes.

There was a bell ringing somewhere in Adele's dream. It was shrill and persistent. She wanted to ignore it, didn't want to wake from her deep, satisfying sleep. Maybe if she did nothing it would stop. But it didn't stop, it went on and on until finally she awoke fully and realised it wasn't in her dream at all—it was her phone ringing. For a moment she thought she was in her room at the hospital but there her pager had been beside her bed and had had a kinder, gentler tone than this one. She sat up in bed, thoroughly confused, struggling through the mists of sleep. And then she remembered. She was in the flat at Woolverton House and the phone that was ringing was on the bureau on the far side of the room. Turning her head, she looked at the illuminated display of her clock radio and saw that it was two-fifteen. Whoever could be calling her at that time? With a muttered exclamation she almost fell out of bed then knocked her knee against the edge of a chair as she stumbled across the room and switched on the light on the bureau. She lifted the receiver. 'Hello?' she mumbled.

'Oh, you *are* awake.' Casey's voice was unmistakable.

'Well, I am now,' she snapped irritably.

'You said you'd like to join me if I got a call.'

'A call?' For a moment she thought he meant a house call but she was confused because she'd understood that Toby was on call that night.

'Yes, the police have just phoned. My services are required down at the station. You said you were interested but if you don't want to come...'

Suddenly she was wide awake. 'Oh, yes,' she said hurriedly. 'Yes, of course. Just let me put some clothes on.'

'Five minutes,' he said. 'I'll meet you downstairs. Wear something warm—we'll take the bike.'

Adele quite literally threw on her clothes—a warm sweater and cord trousers, socks, ankle boots and a thick jacket. What Casey had said was true. She *had* wanted to get involved in his police work, she just hadn't thought it would be quite so soon and when she was so exhausted after her first day in the practice. She was about to leave the flat when, as an afterthought, she grabbed a pair of woollen gloves.

The house was silent and Adele crept along the corridor past Penny's door and down the stairs to the first-floor landing. Peering over the banisters, she could just make out the shape of a figure downstairs in the hallway. She sped down the stairs terrified now that he wouldn't wait, knowing how Casey hated to be kept waiting.

She was slightly breathless when she joined him but he made no comment, simply led the way down the passages to the rear of the house where he unbolted the door and they stepped out into the courtyard. There was a moon that peeped intermittently between the ragged dark clouds that raced across its face. The chill in the air was a shock after the warm September day and while Casey wheeled the bike out of its lockup lean-to Adele pulled up the collar of her jacket and thrust her hands into her pockets.

Without a word he handed her a crash helmet then proceeded to push the motorbike out of the courtyard, under the archway and out into the road. After only a moment's hesitation Adele followed him, fastening the helmet as she went. By the time she joined him at the pavement's edge he was astride the bike.

'Hold onto me,' he ordered abruptly after she had mounted and was sitting squarely behind him. 'I don't want you falling off. I haven't time to come back looking for you.'

Taking a deep breath to quell her irritation, Adele slid her arms around his waist as he turned the key in the ignition and with a slight shudder the big machine purred into life.

It wasn't the first time she'd been on a motorbike. When she and Elaine had been growing up, many holidays had been spent with their Irish cousins in Killarney and several of the boys had owned motorbikes. It had been nothing for a large crowd of them to go into the next town to a club and the bikes had been the only available form of transport. She had enjoyed those rides but that had been all of ten years ago and it felt strange now to feel the steady throb of the engine beneath her. But that was probably where the similarity ended, for those bikes belonging to her cousins had been noisy, smelly contraptions which had seemed to spend as much time in pieces in someone's back yard as on the road, and the one on which she now rode pillion through the night was a thoroughbred amongst bikes, so luxurious it was almost like sitting in an armchair with its chrome trim and the deep gold of its bodywork gleaming in the moonlight.

They met no other traffic on the mile or so journey to the police station on the far side of Stourborne Abbas and this, together with the powerful nature of the engine of the machine, meant that they covered the distance in next to no time. Adele found she was quite disappointed when they drew onto the forecourt of the police station as she had just been starting to really enjoy being on a bike again. But as they dismounted she firmly reminded herself why they were there and it had nothing to do with riding about the countryside in the middle of the night on high-powered motorbikes.

'I'm not sure what this is all about,' said Casey as they climbed the steps to the front entrance of the building. 'Something to do with a break-in in a warehouse, I think. I dare say someone has been injured. I thought it might be a good place for you to start.'

Adele nodded. She didn't know what to say. Her body was still trying to adjust to being evicted from sleep and a warm bed in the middle of the night, only to be hurtled through the cold air then deposited on the deserted steps of a police station.

On entering the station, they were greeted by the duty sergeant who, like everyone else Adele had encountered since arriving in Stourborne Abbas, seemed to know Casey very well.

'What have you got for us?' asked Casey, then, realising that the sergeant was staring at Adele with undisguised interest, said, 'Oh, this is Dr Brooks—she's a trainee at the practice but she's also interested in police work. Adele...' He half turned to her. 'This is Sergeant Alan Munro.'

Adele found her hand encased in a paw-like grip as a

huge smile spread across the face of the man behind the
desk. 'Well, it's nice to meet you, Dr Brooks. Must say,
when I called in our friend Casey I didn't expect him to
have such a charming companion—'

'Yes, all right, Alan,' said Casey impatiently. 'Can we
just get on with it, please?'

'Of course.' The sergeant winked at Adele who found
herself smiling back at him. 'There was a break-in down
at the mobile-phone warehouse. We'd luckily had a tip-
off and our boys were ready for them. There was a bit of
a scuffle and there are a few minor injuries, which need
attending to. There is one of them, however, who appears
to have something else wrong with him. He's been complaining of stomach pains.'

'Perhaps you'd like to have a look at that one, Adele,'
said Casey. 'Don't worry,' he said, catching sight of her
anxious expression, 'the sergeant here will arrange for an
officer to accompany you.'

Moments later Adele was being escorted by a police
officer into one of the remand cells at the rear of the station, while Casey was taken into another farther down the
corridor. As the door clanged shut behind them Adele
knew a moment of nervous panic—this was so unlike anything she had ever had to do before—then as she caught
sight of the young man lying on the narrow bunk, his knees
drawn up to his chest, an expression of agony on his face,
her professionalism took over and she forgot her apprehension. She was a doctor and this was a patient requiring
her help, whatever the circumstances.

'This one's been complaining of stomach pain ever
since we brought him in.' The police officer looked to be
even younger than the man on the bunk. 'You'd better let
the doctor have a look at you,' he added.

The young man briefly raised his head and looked at Adele. 'Where's Casey?' he groaned, 'I want Casey.'

'Dr Casey to you,' said Adele crisply, 'and he's otherwise engaged so you've got me.' She leaned over him and with one hand lifted his wrist and placed her other hand on his forehead. He felt incredibly hot to the touch and his pulse was racing rapidly. 'Where is the pain?' she asked.

'Here.' He indicated the right side of his abdomen. 'And it moves—all over.'

'How long have you had the pain?' Adele perched on the bunk beside him and with his help lifted the grubby T-shirt he was wearing.

'Started this morning,' he muttered. 'Then it went off for a bit. Then it came back during the evening. Since then…it's been agony.'

'Any sickness?'

'Yeah, I threw up in the police van.'

Gently but firmly Adele began examining him, moving her hands across his abdomen. When she reached the lower right side she pressed slightly and as she lifted her hand the young man gave a howl of pain.

'Sorry,' said Adele, 'but I believe I've found what I was looking for.' She glanced up at the police officer standing near the door. 'This man will have to go to hospital,' she said briskly.

'I'll tell the sarge,' he replied dubiously, as if he doubted Adele's authority.

'Yes,' she replied firmly, 'and while you're at it tell him to call an ambulance.' She looked down at the young man again then, seeing the fear in his eyes, gently touched his shoulder. 'It's all right,' she said kindly. 'They'll get you sorted out at the hospital.'

'Can't you give me nothin' for the pain?' he groaned.

'I'm sorry, I can't,' Adele replied. 'You may well be

needing an anaesthetic and if I gave you anything now you would be very sick.' She stood up and as she followed the officer from the room the young man on the bunk curled himself into the foetal position once more. The door shut behind them and as the officer locked it Adele said, 'Was that Flo Procter's son, Stevie, by any chance?'

The officer looked at her in surprise. 'Yes,' he said. 'How did you know that? I thought you were new here.'

'Oh,' she said, 'I am, but there are some situations that don't take a lot of working out.'

CHAPTER FIVE

'IT WAS Flo Procter's son,' Adele told Casey when he emerged from the cells.

'Stevie?' Casey threw her a quick look.

'Yes.' She took a deep breath. 'I've sent for an ambulance or rather I've asked the duty sergeant to send for one.'

'What's wrong with him?' There was a frown on Casey's face now and Adele couldn't help but wonder how he would react to her decision.

'I would say almost certainly appendicitis.'

'I see.' His reply was terse, measured. 'So what led you to that conclusion?'

'He's suffered abdominal pain for most of the day with it eventually settling low down on the right side. He has some fever, pulse is rapid and he's vomited. When I examined him there was rebound pain in the appendix area which was very tender.'

By this time they had reached Reception and the duty sergeant looked up from his desk. 'Ambulance is on its way, Dr Brooks,' he said then he ruined it by throwing a questioning look at Casey and saying, 'That all right with you, Casey?'

'Of course.' To Adele's relief Casey nodded briskly. She wasn't sure what she would have done if he'd questioned her decision or even cancelled the ambulance.

'You don't want to examine him for yourself?'

'Why should I?' Casey gave a light shrug. 'Dr Brooks has made her diagnosis—it's down to A and E now to get him sorted out. One thing we should do, though, is to let Flo Procter know.' He glanced at Adele. 'Maybe you'd like that honour, too?'

'Well…' Adele mentally began bracing herself for such an awesome task.

'Don't worry, I wasn't serious. I wouldn't wish that on anyone.' Casey looked at Alan. 'May I use the phone?'

'Be my guest.' The sergeant indicated the desk phone.

Casey lifted the receiver then paused. 'Has he been charged with anything yet?'

'Not really.' Alan shook his head. 'At this stage he's helping us with our enquiries, although I have to say if he hadn't been taken ill he would have been charged with breaking and entering by now.'

'OK. Fine.' Casey punched out a number and Adele realised he must have known it from memory. As he was waiting for someone in the Procter household to answer the phone, the main doors of the station were flung open and another group of men were marched inside amidst much shouting and swearing and a scuffle that broke out between the men and some of the plain-clothes officers who accompanied them.

'It's like Piccadilly Circus in here tonight,' grumbled Alan. 'And to think this wasn't even my shift. I swapped with Dave Masters because it was his mother-in-law's six-tieth birthday party. He owes me one does our Dave.'

'Flo?' Casey put a hand round his ear to allow him to hear against the noise inside the station. 'It's Casey. I'm down at the station. Stevie's here.' He paused. 'Helping with enquiries is the official line…' He held the phone away from his ear and in spite of the din around them Adele quite clearly heard Flo's shouts of anger.

'There's more, Flo,' Casey went on after a moment. 'I'm afraid Stevie's not well. What? His stomach again. We've sent for an ambulance. No, Dr Brooks examined him. She's pretty certain it's his appendix. They'll be taking him to Stourborne A and E. Can you get there, Flo? Good. OK. I'll speak to you later.' He hung up and turned to Adele. 'Flo and her daughter Tammy are going to get a taxi to the hospital. She said when Stevie's better she's going to kill him.'

'We want him back before that,' said Alan dryly.

Casey turned to Adele. 'Well, I think that's you and me finished here so I guess we'd better salvage what's left of the night. See you, Alan.' He nodded to the desk sergeant.

'Yes, see you, Casey.' Alan paused and looked at Adele. 'Hope we see you again, too, Dr Brooks.'

'I'm sure you will.' It was Casey who answered.

Together they left the building and as they were approaching the bike Casey suddenly chuckled.

'What is it?' Adele threw him a questioning look.

'I was just thinking of poor old Flo.'

'Was she very upset?' asked Adele. By this time they had reached the bike and were securing their helmets once more, and Adele realised she was actually looking forward to the ride home.

'More angry than upset, I think,' Casey replied, pulling on his leather gauntlets. 'Mind you, she should be used to it by now—there's always one or another of her brood in some sort of trouble. I only wish Stevie had stayed around long enough this morning for us to see him. Maybe we could have prevented this.' He mounted the bike and waited for Adele to climb onto the pillion.

'Tell me,' she said, leaning forward slightly over Casey's shoulder so that he could hear her. 'Stevie who?'

He turned his head so that his face was only inches from her own. 'Wonder, I should think,' he murmured then he started the engine.

'Oh, yes, of course.' With a smile Adele slipped her arms around his waist and they purred away into the night.

When they reached Woolverton House Adele waited in the doorway while Casey put the bike away. As he joined her she tried unsuccessfully to hide a yawn.

'Tired?' he said, not unsympathetically.

'Just a bit,' she admitted.

'Well, I guess you've had quite a day. Try and get a bit more sleep now.'

Together they climbed the stairs and when they reached his landing Adele paused for a moment. 'See you later,' she said wearily.

He nodded. 'Goodnight—what's left of it.'

She stumbled up the second flight of stairs, vaguely aware that he stood on his landing, watching her, making no attempt to go to his own flat. At last she reached her own door, opened it, stepped inside then stood for a moment with her back to the door and her eyes closed. Casey was right—it had been quite a day. Opening her eyes, she flicked the light switch and looked at the clock on the wall. The hands stood at four-fifteen. With luck she might be able to grab another three hours of sleep before she need get ready for morning surgery.

It was, however, not to be because, tired as she was, Adele found it incredibly difficult to get back to sleep. Her thoughts were chaotic, ranging from images from the police station—from Stevie's pain to the noise and disruption from the men who had been brought in—to the sensation of riding through the night on that high-powered machine with her arms wrapped tightly around Casey's waist. There had been something so unusual, almost alien about the whole experience that it had stirred something in Adele which now, in retrospect, she recognised as excitement and which, when she thought about it, was ridiculous because it wasn't as if it had been the first time that she'd ridden on a motorbike. If it had been, she would probably have been terrified. So, if it wasn't that, she really couldn't account for this source of excitement.

Maybe, she thought as her digital clock passed five-thirty, it could have been the fact that she was at last being involved in some police work. After all, hadn't that been an ambition for a very long time?

Yes, she thought at last as she tossed and turned, that must be what it was—because really and truly there was nothing else it could have been.

She must have drifted off to sleep at about six o'clock only to be awakened by her alarm at seven. With a groan she buried her head in the pillow, then as thirty seconds later the clock repeated its insistent message she hauled herself out of bed in an attempt to prepare herself to face another day.

News came from the hospital that Stevie had undergone an appendicectomy and Adele suspected that Casey paid a private visit either to the hospital or to see Flo at home.

The remaining days of the week followed a similar pattern to that first day, with Adele sitting in on Casey's surgeries, attending house visits with him and becoming familiar with every aspect of the running of the Woolverton House practice, from nurses' clinics to administration and clerical.

Gradually she was getting to grips with procedures, learning people's names—whether members of staff or patients and their families. Then, at the end of the week, quite casually, as if he were commenting on the weather forecast, Casey informed her without any warning that that afternoon she would be taking her first surgery and that he would be sitting in with her.

She stared at him in astonishment. She had been expecting it to be after the weekend, probably the Monday morning surgery, not the final one on a Friday afternoon.

'Better this one than Monday,' he said, reading her mind. 'This way you won't worry about it all over the weekend.' They had just returned from a couple of house visits and were sitting in the staffroom drinking mugs of coffee. Piles of repeat prescriptions requiring his signature surrounded Casey, while Adele had been leafing through copies of medical magazines, trying to keep abreast of the latest research. 'You happy with that?' he asked as if as an afterthought when Adele remained silent.

'Yes, I suppose so. You just took me by surprise, that's all,' she admitted. 'Like you say, I was expecting Monday...'

'Ah, there's no time like the present. You'll be fine—there's nothing like a fraught Friday afternoon surgery.'

'You make it sound like an ordeal.' Adele looked alarmed.

'Not at all. You wait, it'll be all slight symptoms folk think will exacerbate before Monday.'

In spite of Casey's reassuring words, Adele found she was incredibly nervous as she sat in his consulting room, waiting for her first patient. It was the same room where she had sat beside him on numerous occasions since coming to Stourborne Abbas, the only difference being that now, instead of sitting alongside him, she was sitting at the desk while Casey sat behind her in the corner of the room.

'You're nervous, aren't you?' he said quietly after they had sat in total silence for several minutes.

'Yes,' she admitted at last, 'I suppose I am.'

'You're a doctor, Adele—a fully qualified doctor. You've sat in this room with me for the last week. I promise you, there won't be anything you can't deal with and if there is, don't forget I shall be right here behind you.'

'Maybe that's what scares me.' Adele gave a nervous little laugh, looped her dark hair back behind her ear then looked up sharply as there was a knock at the door. 'Come in,' she called, and the door opened to admit a middle-aged man whose reaction on seeing Adele behind the desk was almost one of suspicion.

Adele took a deep breath. 'Hello,' she said. 'Mr Reynolds, isn't it?'

'That's right.' The man's gaze flickered to Casey.

'I'm Dr Brooks,' Adele went on. 'How can I help you?'

'Well, I've been getting this pain—right here.' The man indicated a point below the centre of his chest at the top of his abdomen, but as he did so he was still looking at Casey.

'What sort of pain is it?' asked Adele.

'I think it's a sort of indigestion pain, but it gets very severe. Last time I had it, which was last night, I was rolling around. My wife gave me some indigestion mixture but it didn't seem to work. In fact, it got worse and went right through to my back. I couldn't seem to get away from it no matter what I did.'

'Does the pain come on after you've eaten?' asked Adele as she turned to the computer screen and studied John Reynolds's medical history.

'Yes, I suppose it does, although sometimes it can be as much as an hour or an hour and a half afterwards.'

'I see from your records you have a history of high blood pressure,' said Adele as she switched to the man's medication chart.

'Yes,' Mr Reynolds nodded. 'I saw Dr Fletcher for that and he prescribed them beta-blockers.'

'I'd like to examine you, Mr Reynolds.' Adele indicated

the adjoining room. 'If you'd like to go into the examination room, take off your jacket and shirt and lie on the couch.'

Casey remained silent as Adele continued to study the patient's records then, taking her stethoscope, she made her way into the examination room where she found John Reynolds lying on the couch. Gently but firmly she carried out a thorough examination of his chest and abdomen, talking to him all the while and asking him to indicate the areas that felt tender to pressure. To complete her examination she checked his heart and blood pressure. When she had finished she straightened up. 'If you would like to get dressed,' she said, 'then come back into the consulting room.'

Casey gave her an enquiring look as she re-entered the room. 'Problems?' he said softly.

'Not really.' She sat down at the desk. 'I'm going to refer him for a gastroscopy and ultrasound but I would also like him to have an ECG today.' She paused, looking at the monitor screen again. 'Can I arrange that on the computer?'

'Yes.' Casey nodded. 'Just go into ''Nurses' Clinics'' and you can see what appointments are available.'

By the time the patient returned to the consulting room Adele had set the chain of events in motion for further investigation of his condition. All that remained was for her to explain to him what would happen.

'Ah, Mr Reynolds, please, come and sit down,' she said gently. 'Now,' she said, 'I would like you to have some tests to try to find out what is causing your pain. I'm going to arrange for you to go to the local hospital to have a gastroscopy.'

'What's that?' John Reynolds frowned, his glance travelling rapidly from Adele to Casey then back to Adele.

'It's a procedure where a tube is passed down into your stomach. Don't worry,' she hastened to add when she saw his expression change from one of suspicion to one of alarm. 'You'll be sedated so you won't know what's going on. I also want you to have an ultrasound, which is a very simple procedure and completely painless but it does tell us anything untoward which may be going on inside you.'

'Will I have to stay in hospital for these?' Mr Reynolds still looked worried.

'No.' Adele hastened to reassure him. 'They can both be carried out in the outpatient department and neither should take very long. I'll write to the hospital and you should receive an appointment through the post. Now, the other thing I would like you to have is an ECG—an electrocardiogram.'

'That's for my heart, isn't it? You don't think it was a heart attack, do you?' The man looked thoroughly alarmed now.

'No,' Adele replied firmly, 'I don't. But in view of your blood-pressure problems I want to make absolutely certain. Don't worry, you can have that done here. I've checked with our nurses' clinic and they have an appointment for later this afternoon at four-fifteen. Could you come back for that?'

'I suppose so.' Mr Reynolds looked bewildered. 'I think I'll go and phone my wife first.'

'I think that's a good idea.' Adele smiled at him. 'And, please, try not to worry. We'll find the problem for you and we'll deal with it. In the meantime I'm going to prescribe a course of tablets that should help to control the symptoms and I would like you to try and stick to a fat-free diet for the time being.'

'What do you mean by fat-free?'

'Animal fats really,' Adele explained. 'Things like butter, cheese, cream or full-fat milk. If you ask at the reception desk on your way out, one of the receptionists will give you a diet sheet which will explain things more fully.' As she finished speaking she tore off the prescription she had just printed out and handed it to him. 'Now, is there anything else you want to ask me?'

'I don't think so, Doctor. I can't think straight at the moment.'

'I'll come along and see you after you've had your ECG,' said Adele with a reassuring smile.

'Right.' John Reynolds nodded. 'Well, thank you, Doctor.'

As the patient left the consulting room Adele glanced at Casey. 'Well, that was hardly a trivial, last-minute Friday afternoon appointment.'

'Absolutely not.' He paused. 'Did you come to any conclusions?'

'I think we're probably looking at gall-bladder disease,' said Adele slowly. 'His abdomen was certainly very tender in that area and the pain and symptoms he was describing seem to point to that, but with his history of hypertension I want to make absolutely certain.'

'You did well.'

It was but slight praise but somehow, and in spite of the fact that she was still acutely aware of Casey's presence in the room, it made her feel more confident to face the next four patients, who ranged from a toddler with severe eczema and a young man with diarrhoea and vomiting to a woman with flu-like symptoms and an elderly man with gout.

By the time she reached the last patient on the list she felt totally at ease with the situation, but as she reached out and pressed the buzzer Casey leaned forward and, peering at the computer screen, sucked in his breath sharply.

'What is it?' Adele frowned.

'Elvira Jackson,' he said. 'Not the easiest way to end a week.'

'Elvira Jackson?' said Adele quickly. 'Where have I heard that name—Elvira?'

'It's OK,' said Casey quickly, as without even the sound of a knock the door was suddenly pushed open 'I'll tell you later.'

A woman stood in the doorway, laden with several bags and plastic carriers. Her age was difficult to determine but she could have been anywhere between thirty-five and forty-five. Her long, straggly, dark hair was streaked with grey, her eyes were strangely light-coloured and in spite of the warmth of the September afternoon she was dressed in a grey, ankle-length knitted coat over a long skirt of the same colour with several dark-coloured scarves wound around her neck.

'Hello, Elvira.' It was Casey who spoke first, which surprised Adele for until then he had remained silent as each new patient had entered the room, allowing her to conduct the consultation.

'Who's she?' Those curiously coloured eyes moved to Adele.

'This is Dr Brooks.' Again it was Casey who spoke and Adele decided it was high time she intervened.

'How can I help you?' she asked firmly.

'I'm pregnant,' the woman declared as she dumped the various bags she was carrying onto the floor and sat heavily down on a chair.

'You know that isn't true, Elvira.' Again Casey intervened.

'I might be. I want a test.'

'Very well,' Adele said soothingly. She was beginning to get a little irritated with Casey's interruptions. Either she was taking this surgery or she wasn't. 'I'll give you a specimen pot and you can bring in an early morning sample and we'll have it tested for you,' she went on firmly, ignoring Casey's apparent attempts to attract her attention.

The woman shot a triumphant expression towards Casey as Adele handed her a specimen pot.

'Now, is there anything else?' asked Adele.

Elvira shook her head then stood up and gathered up her bags. Making no attempt to leave the room, she continued staring at Adele. 'I know you,' she said at last.

'Do you?' Adele was a little taken aback by something in the woman's attitude and at the same time conscious of a sudden, unexpected feeling of discomfort which she immediately tried to dismiss. She was a doctor, wasn't she, for heaven's sake? And if she was going to be a GP she had to get used to all types of people and every possible situation that could present itself.

'You're the one who's living in my flat.' The woman's tone was dull, devoid now of the passion that had been in her voice when she'd announced that she was pregnant. Before Adele could respond she turned and without another word walked out of the room.

Adele turned to Casey. 'What did she mean?' she said uneasily as the door clicked shut.

'She's the one who was living in your flat before you,' Casey replied simply.

'The troublemaker?' Adele raised her eyebrows as she recalled the comments Casey had made when he'd first shown her up the stairs to her flat.

'One and the same.' He gave a little shrug.

'In what way was she a troublemaker?' Suddenly Adele needed to know.

Casey sighed and Adele gained the impression that he was reluctant to talk about Elvira Jackson. 'Let's just say it was a mistake in the first place to allow her to have use of the flat.'

'So who's fault was that? Who was responsible?'

'Unfortunately it was Toby,' Casey admitted. 'Elvira was his patient. She has a long history of psychiatric problems, together with a personality disorder. When she was evicted from her previous flat Toby felt sorry for her and told her she could stay temporarily in the flat, which is now yours. When the local council found alternative accommodation for her she didn't want to move out. We had to get a bit tough in the end.'

'But in what way was she a troublemaker?' Adele frowned.

'She has some very strange ways. For a start she has a fascination with fire. We didn't know that until after she'd moved in and left candles burning which set fire to the curtains and almost burned the whole place down.'

'But surely that could have been an accident,' Adele protested.

'She also developed a fixation with Toby,' Casey went on calmly. 'She followed him everywhere, wouldn't leave him alone. On one occasion she even parked herself in his examination room and stayed there while he took a surgery. He didn't know she was there until a patient went in to get undressed—it quite unnerved him.'

'Yes, I'm sure it did, but—'

'On another occasion she started sending anonymous mail to the reception staff, accusing them of heaven knows what, then sticking up posters in the waiting room listing things they were supposed to be doing.'

'Were the police involved?'

'Only in a very superficial way. Elvira is well known to

the police, unfortunately because of her medical conditions. There seems to be little that can be done apart from warnings…but she appears to be reasonably harmless. Strange maybe, but harmless.'

'Is she still registered with Toby?' asked Adele slowly.

'No, she's with Jeanette now. We thought it for the best to move her. You probably only got her today because I'm duty doctor and she was an extra.' Casey leaned back in his chair. 'Maybe we should have removed her from the list entirely but if we did it would mean she would have to travel miles to another practice.'

'Why did you think she couldn't be pregnant?' asked Adele curiously.

'Because in the past she's had two terminations, which have left her infertile.'

'Oh.' She stared at Casey. 'Why didn't you say? I feel a fool now, telling her to do a specimen.'

Casey shrugged. 'I was going to stop you then I thought it was probably best to humour her—let her have what she wanted.'

'But does she seriously think she could be pregnant?' Adele stared at him in concern. 'If so, I find that incredibly sad.'

'Yes, it is. But with Elvira, who knows? Unfortunately, anything is possible.'

'Doesn't she have a psychiatric social worker?'

'Yes, she does, a young woman by the name of Ruby Felton who monitors Elvira and who on the whole does a good job with her because most of the time she's OK—it's just when she gets some sort of fixation that the trouble starts.'

'Like with Toby, you mean?'

'Yes, poor old Toby—he didn't know what had hit him.'

Casey sighed and stood up. 'Well, that looks like the end of your first surgery,' he said. 'How are you feeling?'

'All right,' Adele replied. 'But I think there's going to be much more to being a GP than I had ever realised…it's going to be a real challenge.'

'Think you'll rise to it?' He raised his eyebrows and the scar on his face stood out sharply, making Adele once again want to ask him how he had got it.

'Oh, yes,' she said firmly. 'I have no doubts about that.'

CHAPTER SIX

'I'VE been called out. Want to come along?'

'Yes, of course.' It was Sunday afternoon and Adele was in her bathroom, having just washed her hair, but she didn't hesitate when she took Casey's call on her mobile phone. 'Give me five minutes,' she said.

As she left her flat she met Penny on the landing.

'Oh, there you are,' said Penny. 'I was just coming to see you. I wondered if you fancied strolling down to the pub for a swift half.'

'Penny, I'm sorry, I can't—' Adele began.

'Never mind,' Penny cut her short. 'How about a quick coffee? It won't take me long, the kettle has just boiled.'

'No, you don't understand,' Adele explained. 'I have to go out right away. Casey has had a call-out.'

'And you're going with him.' It wasn't a question, more a resigned statement.

'Well, yes—he's just phoned and suggested I might like to go.'

'I see.' A tight, almost shuttered expression had come across Penny's face. 'Well, not to worry. Some other time.'

'Yes, some other time,' Adele agreed hastily. 'I'd like that.' Edging past the other woman, she added, 'I'm sorry but I must fly…' She found herself almost apologising for the fact that she was going out with Casey, which was utterly ridiculous because, no matter what there might be between Casey and Penny, Casey was her trainer and this was her job. She fled down the stairs, aware that Penny was still watching her. Hurrying through the house and out into the courtyard, she found Casey sitting in the Land Rover with the engine running.

'It's a police call,' he explained as she climbed in beside him, 'and in view of the fact of where it is I decided the Land Rover would be more sensible than the bike.' They drew out of the courtyard and onto the main road where there was very little traffic as most of the high street shops were closed on a Sunday.

'Your hair is wet,' Casey observed after driving in silence for a while.

'It'll soon dry.' She shrugged.

'You don't have to come with me every time, you know. It isn't compulsory.'

'I know. I want to come. It's the only way I'm going to build up any experience.'

'Fair enough. I just didn't want it said that I was putting you under any undue pressure, that's all.'

'Has anyone said that?' Adele turned and looked at him but his expression as he studied the road ahead was implacable. He was casually dressed today in jeans and a sweatshirt and she was glad that she, too, was similarly clad.

'Penny suggested you might have too much on your plate,' he replied.

Adele frowned, irritated. 'What does it have to do with Penny?' she asked.

'Nothing.' He raised his shoulders. 'I suppose she just knows that I can be a bit of a slave-driver, that's all.'

And Penny would know that, of course. Penny would know him better than most. She took a deep breath, dismissing Penny from her mind but troubled slightly by their recent encounter, although she couldn't say why. She also found once again that even the thought of Penny and Casey together disturbed her. 'Where are we going?' she asked in a concerted effort to change the subject.

'To an old chalk quarry,' he replied. 'It's about five miles out of town up towards Langstone Ridge. It's pretty rough terrain up there.'

'Do we know what it's all about?'

He nodded. 'The police have recovered a body.' He said it in the same matter-of-fact tone he might have used if he'd been asked to comment on the weather.

'Oh.' She threw him a startled glance. Somehow it was the last thing she'd expected to hear.

'I am needed to certify the death.'

'I see.' She fell silent, reflecting on what he had just said. After a while she said, 'Do you think this could be anything to do with the missing girl that has been on the news in the last few days?'

'It's possible,' Casey replied. 'But one of the things that I've learnt in this business is never to jump to conclusions.'

They travelled in silence for some distance then as if he, too, was attempting to change the subject, he said, 'Have you heard about Edward's and Celia's dinner party?'

'Yes,' Adele dragged her mind from missing girls and bodies being found in chalk quarries. 'Celia phoned last night and invited me. She said it was by way of a welcome to me.'

Casey gave a sound, which could have been a grunt.

'Will you go?' she asked him curiously.

'Dinner parties are definitely not my cup of tea but I guess on this occasion I will have to make an exception.'

'Do you think all the staff will be there?'

'I shouldn't think so—just the partners and their spouses, I would imagine, and possibly Rachel and her husband.'

'I see.' Adele wondered if that included Penny because, although not a spouse, at staff social events she well could be included as Casey's partner. She could have asked him, she supposed, but found she didn't want to. Turning her head, she gazed out of the window. The sky was darkening, with rain clouds rolling in from the west and a light drizzle already beginning to mist the windscreen. She wished she'd had the sense to check the weather and to take a rain jacket instead of rushing headlong from the flat. They had left the town far behind now. Travelling in the opposite direction from the Bowscombe Estate, they seemed to be climbing steadily through a thickly wooded area where the closeness of the trees made the afternoon light appear darker than it already was.

'This is a pretty isolated area up here,' observed Casey as they emerged from the trees. 'In the summer it can be quite spectacular with a chance to see plenty of wildlife, but on a day like this it's grim to say the least.' As if to reinforce his words, great gusts of rain began driving across the vast open area of scrubland, obscuring their vision and making driving conditions hazardous.

'The quarries are somewhere over there.' Casey narrowed his eyes and peered across to their left where amidst a mass of rocks and bushes a flashing blue light could be seen. 'Yes, this is it. There are the police. Hold tight, this could get bumpy.' Leaving the road, they drove across the rough, rocky ground and as they entered the bushes a policeman appeared in front of the vehicle indicating for them to stop.

Casey wound down the window and the rain lashed through the opening, spraying both him and Adele.

'Hello, Casey.' The officer nodded. 'I thought that was you.'

'Julian.' Casey nodded in reply. 'Who's in charge?'

'Detective Inspector Daniels,' the officer replied, peering past Casey at Adele.

'It's OK,' Casey said. 'This is Dr Brooks, my trainee.'

'Right. I'll take you down there. You'd better walk from here. It's very rough going.'

Casey turned to Adele. 'Have you got a coat?' he asked.

'No.' She was almost ashamed to admit that she had been foolish enough not to come prepared for any eventuality. Anticipating his disdain, she added, 'It doesn't matter—I'll just get wet.'

'Don't be ridiculous,' he snapped. 'You'll catch your death. Here, take this.' Leaning back, he retrieved his waxed jacket from the rear of the vehicle and tossed it to her.

'But what about you?' she asked helplessly.

'There's an old oilskin there—I'll use that,' he muttered. 'What have you got on your feet?'

Fortunately she had pulled on a pair of boots before leaving the flat so was able to say, 'It's OK, I'm wearing boots.'

He made a noise that could have been a grunt of approval and when she jumped down from the vehicle she saw that he, too, was wearing stout leather walking boots. The rain hit them immediately, taking Adele's breath away, and as they began following the policeman across the wild scrubland the only sound to be heard was the moaning of the wind in the distant trees. If Adele's hair had started to dry since leaving the flat it was wet again in seconds, sticking to her head as the rain ran down her face in rivulets.

Two police recovery vehicles were parked amongst the bushes around the edge of the quarry, and a green tarpaulin had been erected behind the vehicles to form a makeshift tent. Uniformed police, accompanied by Alsatian dogs, were searching the area while the plain-clothes officers in the back of one of the vehicles emerged only when they caught sight of Casey and Adele.

'Hello, Melvin.' Casey nodded to one of the officers, a tall, thin man with red hair and a pale, freckled complexion who looked as if he'd rather have been anywhere else in the world than at this rain-swept quarry on a Sunday afternoon, dealing with whatever tragedy lay beyond the green tarpaulin.

'Afternoon, Casey.' DI Daniels glanced at Adele.

'This is Dr Brooks,' Casey explained. 'She's my trainee.'

'Does she want to be in on this?' DI Daniels eyed Adele doubtfully.

'Of course.' It was Adele who briskly replied.

'As you wish.' The detective gave a slight shrug as if to say that it was up to her but that she'd been warned.

'What have we got?' asked Casey as they began to follow the detective towards the tarpaulin.

'The body of a young girl,' Melvin Daniels replied. 'And before you ask, yes, it does look very much like it's the teenager who's been missing for the last couple of weeks.' Lifting the flap of the tent, he stood back to allow them to enter ahead of him.

It would have been gloomy in the tent but the police had set up an arc light, which cast a pool of light directly onto a shockingly small bundle on the ground. The body was lying beneath a plastic sheet and as DI Daniels crouched down and lifted the sheet, Adele braced herself for whatever she might be about to see. In her work as a hospital doctor she had seen death on many occasions but usually it had been as a result of illness, of natural causes or from an accident. She had never seen death as the result of violence or murder.

The girl was lying on her side almost in the foetal position and looked young, very young, little more than a child really with her pale, blue-tinged face and her wispy blonde hair matted and caked with mud. Taking over from the detective, Casey gently drew back the plastic sheet that covered her body and Adele caught a glimpse of a pink and orange striped T-shirt. The sight of it struck a chord with her and she realised it was identical to one she had bought for Elaine's daughter Holly on her last birthday. As her stomach lurched in revolt Adele's gaze flew again to the girl's face. This girl was fair; Holly was dark. It wasn't Holly but the thought that it might have been and that she was someone's daughter, someone's niece, was Adele's undoing.

Gagging, she turned abruptly away, leaving Casey to do what he had to do. Stumbling outside, past DI Daniels, she collided with one of the officers.

'Are you all right, miss?' He was an older man, big, burly and somehow reassuring as he held her by her arms, steadying her.

'Yes,' Adele gasped. 'Yes, thanks, I'm fine.' She wasn't fine, she felt dreadful, but she could hardly say as much.

'Not pleasant, is it?' The officer jerked his head in the direction of the tarpaulin that concealed its tragic burden.

'No.' Adele gulped, breathing in great breaths of the cold damp air in an effort to steady herself. 'No, it isn't.'

'Your first time, is it?' asked the officer sympathetically.

Adele nodded, suddenly unable to trust her voice. Thrusting her hands into the pockets of her jacket, it took her a full minute to realise that this was, in fact, not her jacket but Casey's, and that the objects inside, the scraps of paper, the pen, the set of keys, weren't hers. Almost guiltily she withdrew her hands.

Casey emerged a few minutes later and Adele found she

was unable to meet his gaze. She waited in the gusting rain as he climbed into the back of one of the police vehicles, presumably to complete essential paperwork. By the time he joined her she had managed to pull herself together at least enough to face the somewhat uncompromising stare of the detective inspector.

'Thanks, Casey.' Melvin Daniels nodded then glanced at Adele. 'You OK, Dr Brooks?'

'Yes, fine,' Adele lied. She was far from fine but she didn't want him or any of his men or even Casey, come to that, to know just how badly she had been affected.

In silence they walked back to the Land Rover, and as Casey unlocked her door she almost fell inside and thankfully sank down into her seat. It was a relief to get out of the wind and the rain but more than that it was as if the familiarity of the vehicle offered some sanctuary from the grim reality of what had happened.

Casey sat for a moment with his hands resting on the steering-wheel, making no attempt to start the engine as if he, too, had been deeply affected by what he had witnessed. 'I'm sorry,' he said at last, turning his head to look at Adele.

'Wh-what d-do you m-mean?' To her horror her teeth were chattering as she tried to speak.

'I shouldn't have taken you there. It was too much, too soon. I should have realised what it might have been.'

'Y-you said you c-can't take anything f-for g-granted.'

'I know, but I should have anticipated.'

'She'd b-been murdered, hadn't she?' In her anxiety Adele began twisting her cold wet hands together.

'It looked that way.' Casey took a deep breath and started the engine.

'How?' Adele's voice was little more than a whisper

and for a moment she thought he might not have heard her above the sound of the engine.

But as they bumped over the rough terrain and the windscreen wipers began to whirr again he shook his head. 'That wasn't for me to say. The post-mortem will determine that.'

'But—' Adele wanted to say that he must have seen signs, must have known or suspected, but he cut her short.

'My job was simply to certify the death. It's best not to speculate, Adele. Believe me, I know. If you start speculating you'll drive yourself mad.'

They were silent after that as Casey drove through the wind and the rain back to Woolverton House. By the time they arrived it was almost dark, and after Casey had parked the Land Rover they made their way through the house and up the stairs. As they reached the first-floor landing Adele would have left Casey and carried on up to her own floor but he touched her arm, stopping her.

'Oh,' she said. 'Your coat—sorry.'

'No, it isn't that.' He indicated the closed door to his flat. 'Come in for a moment.'

She didn't want to. She wanted to get back to her own flat, peel off her wet clothes and step into a hot bath, but somehow he didn't give her the chance to refuse and she found herself meekly waiting as he unlocked the door. As the door swung open Adele glanced up the stairs, wondering what Penny would think if she saw her going into Casey's flat with him, but to her relief there was no sign of Penny and the door to her flat was firmly closed.

The door swung open then Casey flicked the light switch and stood back, allowing Adele to precede him into the flat. It was larger than her apartment, she could see that at a glance, but it was tastefully furnished if in a rather minimalist masculine way with dark wood furniture and a large, glass-topped coffee-table between two leather sofas.

'Let me relieve you of that coat.' Casey slipped the waxed jacket from her shoulders and, together with the oilskin he was wearing, took it through to what appeared to be the kitchen. He reappeared almost immediately, carrying a large, white towel. 'Here,' he said, handing it to her. 'Get yourself dry.'

She stared at him and for the moment it seemed as if she was rooted to the spot, incapable of action.

'Adele…?' he said gently, bending his head slightly to look into her face. To her horror her eyes filled with tears and she was forced to press one hand to her mouth to quell the sob that suddenly threatened to erupt. With a quiet exclamation he reached out and, putting his hand beneath her chin, tilted her face up to his. 'Hey,' he said softly, his eyes curiously tender. 'What is this…?'

'I'm sorry,' she whispered as the tears began to run unchecked down her face. 'It's just that…the girl…she was wearing a T-shirt identical to one that I gave my niece for her birthday…' She gulped, the tears suddenly choking her. 'She…she didn't look much older than Holly… I keep thinking it could have been her. And it was so awful up there, so wet and wild…and…and so lonely…' She shook her head in distress, unable to blot out the pictures that filled her head.

Without a word Casey stepped forward and before Adele had a chance to even think what he was doing he put his arms around her and held her close, so close that all she could hear was the steady beating of his heart through the damp fabric of his sweatshirt as he allowed her tears to flow.

It felt safe, warm and secure in the shelter of his arms and at that moment, if she'd been asked, Adele quite easily could have said that she was happy to stay there indefinitely. But gradually, inevitably, common sense began to return and Adele was the first to move.

'I'm sorry,' she muttered as she fumbled for a tissue, wiping both her eyes and blowing her nose. 'That was very unprofessional of me.'

'Not at all.' He didn't release her, just moved back a bit so he could look into her face again while keeping his arms around her. He really should let her go, she thought, albeit half-heartedly, but he didn't. Instead, he said, 'It wasn't unprofessional at all. It was a perfectly normal, human reaction to tragedy and violence. I just wish I'd thought it through before I allowed you to go in there.'

'I have to get used to that sort of thing if I'm going to be involved in police work,' Adele protested weakly.

'That's true,' he admitted, 'but there are ways of preparing you and I guess I neglected them.'

Still he made no attempt to release her and by this time Adele was beginning to feel not only embarrassed at the way she had shown her weakness and her vulnerability but also uncomfortable at the way she must look. She was cold and wet and could feel that her hair was plastered to her head. And if that wasn't enough, she had been crying— her nose always turned red when she cried. And as it finally dawned on her just how unattractive she must appear she finally managed to pull away from him. Picking up the towel which had somehow fallen to the floor, she began to dry her hair and face while Casey, after watching her for a moment, disappeared into the kitchen then returned to stand in the doorway, vigorously drying his own hair with a dark red towel.

'Are your clothes wet?' he asked after a few moments.

'No,' she replied hastily. 'They're fine.' Her jeans, in fact, were quite damp but she had no doubt that if she'd said yes he would have had no qualms in telling her to take them off so that he could dry them. 'That jacket kept me really dry.'

With the red towel draped casually around his neck, Casey strolled back into the room, crouched down in front of the fireplace and lit the gas fire. 'Come and get warm,' he said as the comforting glow from the flames flickered around the room.

Adele perched on the edge of one of the leather sofas while Casey crossed to a cabinet on the far side of the room, opened it and took out two glasses and a bottle.

A moment later he returned with the glasses and handed one to her. 'Brandy,' he said firmly. 'It'll do you good. You've had a shock.'

She didn't drink spirits very often, preferring to stick to wine, but on this occasion she made no protest and as she sipped the amber-coloured liquid and the combined warmth from that and the fire began to steal through her veins she slowly felt herself begin to recover.

Casey sat opposite her and, taking a mouthful of his own brandy, cradled the glass in his hand. 'Tell me about your niece,' he said after a while.

'Her name is Holly,' Adele replied, setting her glass down on the coffee-table. 'She's my sister Elaine's oldest child and she's twelve years old. She's...she's great,' she added, 'and I love her to bits.'

'You say she's your sister's eldest child?'

'Yes, Elaine has two other children—Katy who's nine and Harry who's five.'

'So is Elaine your only sister?' He sounded as if he was really interested, as if he wanted to know, and suddenly Adele felt something wash over her that could only be described as homesickness. Maybe it was a direct result of the events of the afternoon, she didn't know, but whatever it was she found herself moving farther back on the sofa, settling herself more comfortably, at ease now as she talked of her family.

'Yes,' she said, 'there are just the two of us. Elaine is four years older than me.'

'So she started her family when she was very young,' he observed.

'She did,' Adele agreed. 'She started training to be a teacher, then she met Rod—he's a solicitor—they married within a year and Elaine very soon found she liked having babies.'

'And what about you?' He raised an eyebrow, the one split by the scar, which in the subdued lighting of the room somehow gave him a slightly demonic look.

'What about me?' she said quickly, wondering to what he was referring.

'Don't you think you would like having babies?'

'I don't know.' She shrugged. 'I knew first and foremost I wanted to be a doctor and I guess that took precedence.'

'You can have both these days,' he observed.

'You sound like my mother.' Adele wrinkled her nose. 'She's always going on about the fact that being a doctor shouldn't automatically bar me from settling down and having a family, thus presenting her with more grandchildren, of course.'

'And I guess that could well have happened if everything had gone according to plan with Nigel,' said Casey quietly.

'What?' She looked up sharply, slightly shocked at the sound of Nigel's name on Casey's lips. 'Oh, yes,' she said slowly, remembering that he knew about Nigel because it had been her who had told him. 'Yes, I guess so. I think my mother thought Nigel was a highly suitable prospective son-in-law. Just shows how wrong she was, doesn't it?'

she added. There was a hint of bitterness in her tone but to her surprise not as much as there once had been. Maybe she was becoming immune to the pain she'd once felt whenever she'd thought of Nigel.

Fortified by this thought, she took another sip of brandy. Looking across at Casey, she said, 'How about you? Does your mother go on at you to settle down again and have a family?'

He didn't answer and abruptly Adele set her glass down. 'Oh, heavens,' she said, 'I've done it again. Your mother isn't alive, is she?'

'No, as it happens, she isn't,' he admitted, then as her expression changed, he said, 'But don't go apologising again. It happened a long time ago, when I was in my early teens, in fact.'

'So what happened to you afterwards? Did your father bring you up?'

'My parents had divorced but, yes, after my mother died my brother and I went to live with our father. We lived in a very tough neighbourhood and most of the time we lived by our wits.'

'So when did you decide you wanted to be a doctor?' Suddenly Adele was curious. As she knew only too well, it took time, money and dedication to become a doctor and it didn't sound as if Casey's background was indicative of any of these.

'It had been my mother's dream that I should become a doctor and that my brother should study law. For a long time I simply wasn't interested—it all seemed too much like hard work and I was far happier hanging out with a local gang and getting up to Lord knows what rather than applying myself to study. The school I attended wasn't much use either and there was no real encouragement to try to better myself.'

'So what changed?' asked Adele.

'Ironically it was my mother's death that did it. She was only in her thirties. It was breast cancer—they didn't have the facilities or resources that they do today and she died within a year.' He paused and stared down into his glass. 'It gutted me, I don't mind telling you,' he went on after a while. 'I was rebellious, I didn't want to go and live with my dad, didn't want to leave my mates. I even said I didn't want to leave the school I was going to, even though I hated it, but the alternative would have been going into care, and I didn't want that either, so in the end I didn't really have a lot of choice.'

'So was it not as bad as you thought in the end?'

'Oh, it was tough, make no mistake about that—a father I hardly knew, a stepmother I viewed with distrust and a new school where I was viewed with distrust because I was an outsider. As you can imagine, it wasn't exactly a picnic.'

'So what happened?' She was intensely curious now. 'How did you get from that to where you are today as a partner in a firm of GPs in a county market town?'

He allowed that rare smile to touch his features as he considered his reply. 'Two things,' he said. 'A teacher began to take an interest in me and led me to believe that if I wanted something enough I could have it.'

'And the second?' she asked quietly, somehow knowing what was coming.

'I suppose if I'm honest,' he said, 'I knew deep down that I could do it and I decided I owed it to my mum to do so.'

CHAPTER SEVEN

'SHE would have been proud of you,' said Adele softly.

'I hope so.' Casey took another mouthful of his drink and stared into the fire as if lost in memories from his past. To Adele he suddenly looked vulnerable, not a bit like the tough-guy image she had come to associate with Casey, and she had to fight an urge to sink down onto her knees beside him and put her arms around him.

Instead, as the urge subsided, gently she said, 'And what about your family now?'

'How do you mean?' He raised his head and looked at her.

'Well, your father—where is he?'

'He's in a residential home—I visit him when I can.'

'And his wife?'

'The marriage didn't last.' His reply was brief, abrupt almost, and Adele sensed this was an area he didn't want to talk about.

'And what about your brother—did he study law?'

'Oh, yes,' said Casey softly, peering into his glass as he spoke, 'he studied law.'

'So your mum would have been proud of him as well.'

'Well, that's debatable.' He looked up and his gaze met Adele's. 'The way he studied the law ended up with a spell in prison.'

'Oh, dear.' She paused. 'And now?'

'We've rather lost touch but it would never surprise me to hear he's back behind bars.'

Adele remained silent for a while because there really

didn't seem any more to say on the subject. In the end it was Casey who broke the silence.

'Are you feeling better?' he asked.

'Yes, much, thank you. In fact, I really should think about going…'

'Why?'

'Well, I'm sure you have things to do, and I, well, I—'

'Are you warm?' he asked interrupting her.

'Yes.'

'And comfortable?'

'Oh, yes.'

'Then stay awhile. There's no need to rush off.'

'All right,' she said weakly. She knew she should go really. She had things to do. On the other hand, what she'd just told Casey was true—she was warm and comfortable sitting there on his sofa in front of the fire, sipping brandy and talking about their families, their lives. But there was more than that. There was the lingering memory of how it had been when his arms had gone around her and she'd felt safe and protected. And maybe that was the most telling reason why she should go. It had felt good in his arms but she had had no right to feel that way any more than she'd had any right to be there in the first place. No, there really were no two ways about it—she should go.

But still she sat there, relaxed and contented, as it grew darker outside, the rain lashed against the windows and the wind howled in the chimney.

'The girl,' she said at last. 'Was she one of our patients?'

Casey shook his head. 'No, she wasn't registered here. And I have to say I'm relieved about that. Probably at this very moment some other poor GP is having to deal with hysterical parents.'

'I don't know how people recover from something like that,' said Adele slowly.

'I don't think people ever do fully recover from the death of a child,' he replied. 'I guess they simply learn to live with the pain.' He paused. 'I never knew my daughter,' he went on after a moment, 'but when she was born, I saw her and held her and I can honestly say I don't think a day goes by that I don't think about her...' He shook his head and as Adele caught the glint of unshed tears in his eyes she had the distinct impression that this was the first time that he'd spoken like this to anyone and once again she had to fight the urge to put her arms around him.

'But this...' he went on after a moment, 'this is different. To lose a child in this terrible way as the result of violence...well, that's something else...' He gave a gesture of hopelessness that implied the whole thing would be beyond him. Then, in an obvious attempt to change the subject and at the same time supposedly to regain his composure, he hauled himself to his feet. 'Let me make you some coffee,' he said.

'No, really.' Adele also rose to her feet. 'I must be going. I have things to do before tomorrow. Why...' She managed a weak smile. 'Before I know where I am it'll be time for morning surgery and I shall be behind that desk again.'

She began to make her way to the door but somehow he got there before her and stood there barring her way.

She looked up at him, trying to read the expression in his eyes as he looked steadily back at her, but found it impossible. All she knew was that she'd seen the expression before on several occasions but most notably at the moment when they'd first met.

'Casey...?' she said softly, and all she could think of then was that the last time she had been this close to him he had put his arms around her and held her, and quite suddenly she knew that was exactly what she wanted to happen again. She found herself carefully scrutinising his face, from those dark, brooding eyes, the rugged features and the scar to the dark shadow of stubble on his jaw.

'Casey…?' she whispered again. As she became aware of some battle that seemed to be raging behind his eyes she reached out her hand and with the tips of her fingers gently traced the line of the scar all the way from where it divided his eyebrow down the side of his face to where it ended at the corner of his jawbone. 'Tell me,' she said, about to ask him how he had come by such a scar, but that was as far as she got for with a sound that could quite easily have been a groan, and for the second time that evening, he put his arms around her.

It felt the same, just as good, safe, warm and comforting as before. The smell of him was the same, a slightly woody smell, and he felt the same, the same hard muscular body through the fabric of his sweatshirt. But that was where the similarities ended, for on the previous occasion his motive had presumably been simply to console, to comfort. This time there was urgency, almost a roughness about the way his arms tightened around her, which touched a chord somewhere deep inside and she found herself spontaneously lifting her face to his.

His kiss was hard and firm and so full of passion it took Adele's breath away, leaving her gasping and at first yearning for more. Then, as his hands became entangled in her hair and his kiss grew deeper and more demanding, she felt shocked at her own response.

In the end it was she who drew away. 'Casey,' she murmured. 'We mustn't…'

He appeared not to hear her at first as if so driven by passion and desire that he was oblivious to any sort of reason, and it was only when she put her hands on his chest and gently pushed him away from her that he appeared to return to his senses.

'What…?' He stared at her, confusion in his eyes as desire ebbed away.

'I said…we mustn't,' she said shakily.

And then as it seemed to dawn on him for the first time what they had done he appeared to visibly shake himself. 'No,' he said abruptly, 'no, of course not. I'm sorry, Adele. That shouldn't have happened.'

'It's all right.' She attempted to straighten her hair, to push it back from her face. 'I really think I should go.'

'Yes, of course.' Casey stood aside, running a hand over his own short dark hair, the gesture helpless and yet at the same time somehow boyish.

'I…I'll see you in the morning,' said Adele, her voice husky, not like her voice at all. He nodded, seeming now to be incapable of speech. Putting her head down, suddenly unable to face what might be in his eyes, she tugged open the door and fled out of his flat and up the stairs.

Mercifully there was no sign of Penny. Adele really didn't think she could have coped if she'd met her on the landing and been forced to answer questions about where she and Casey had been. Once in her own flat she ran a bath, added a generous amount of bath foam and, peeling off her clothes, stepped into the comforting warmth of the water.

She was still in a state of turmoil over what had happened between herself and Casey and it was a turmoil that was to last for the rest of the evening, long after she'd had her bath, prepared supper—only to find that she had lost her appetite—watched some television, without being able to say what she had seen, then finally taken herself off to bed. What had happened had been a shock and yet, on the other hand, there had been a sort of inevitability about it—almost as if, now that she looked back on it, both of them had somehow been waiting for it to happen and that it had only been a matter of time before it had.

But it had been wrong. They both knew that and there was no telling where it might have ended, although Adele had a pretty shrewd suspicion. She had protested, not because she didn't find him attractive but because of his involvement with Penny, and Casey himself had said it shouldn't have happened.

So why had he let it happen? If he had restrained himself she wouldn't now be feeling as wretched as she did. Was it quite simply that all men were the same and when it came to restraint they were incapable, or to fidelity where they thought that if no one found out it didn't matter? That had happened with Nigel. He had thought as long as Adele and Lucinda didn't find out about each other no one would get hurt. He had calmly assumed he could have his cake and eat it as well. Was that what Casey thought, too?

Maybe it was, maybe it wasn't. All Adele knew was that he wasn't going to get the chance to find out. She finally fell asleep that night after firmly resolving to ignore the powerful emotions he had stirred in her, emotions all the more disturbing because they had surfaced so abruptly after recently having lain dormant. But more disquieting than all of that, and uppermost in her mind before sleep claimed her, was the fact that the emotions and desires evoked by Casey made a pale shadow out of what she'd felt for Nigel.

The following morning found Adele very apprehensive about taking surgery with Casey but in the end she need have had no such worries for he acted as if nothing had happened between them, bidding her good morning and taking his place slightly behind her in his consulting room as Lizzie brought in the bundle of patient records and placed them on the desk.

She, however, was acutely aware of him—the sight of him in the casual chinos and sweater that he invariably chose to wear for surgery, his hair still damp from the shower, that woody smell that must be the aftershave he used and his very presence that seemed to fill the small room. In spite of her strong resolutions of the night before, she found herself longing for him to take her into his arms again just as he had then, for those strong hands resting now on the computer keyboard to touch her and for his mouth to take control of hers...

But, of course, he did nothing of the sort—that would never happen again.

'Good morning, Doctor.'

Shaken from her reverie, Adele looked up sharply at the woman who had just come into the room and who was lowering herself gingerly onto the chair.

'Good morning...Mrs...er...Mrs Bletchford. How can I help you?'

'Well, Doctor, I keep getting this funny pain...'

Within minutes Adele was drawn into the complexities of yet another daily surgery, but in spite of the fact that she was required to use every ounce of her concentration she remained only too aware of the presence of the man at her side.

As the surgery wore on she found herself wondering what Casey would say when the surgery ended and they were alone. Would he make any reference to what had happened between them, would he maybe attempt to apologise or explain his actions? But she was destined never to know because as she was printing out a prescription for the morning's last patient a telephone call came through.

Handing the patient the prescription and bidding him good-bye, Adele lifted the receiver, noting as she did so that it was an internal call.

'Adele—it's Penny. We have a lady in the clinic—Marion Kendry—whom I'm very concerned about. She has a history of heart problems. She came in for a routine ECG but she's complaining of feeling unwell. She's Casey's patient—is he there?'

'Yes, he is.'

'Can you ask him to come along to the clinic, please?'

'Of course.' Adele looked at the receiver as Penny cut her short and hung up.

'What is it?' Casey raised his eyebrows. The one bisected by the scar looked ruffled and suddenly, irrationally, she longed to touch it, to smooth it as she had before. But even if that was permitted, which now quite obviously it wasn't, there were other, more pressing matters to attend to.

'Penny wants you in the clinic,' she said. 'A patient of yours, Marion Kendry…?'

Casey nodded. 'Yes, what about her?'

'She's feeling unwell. Penny is worried about her in view of her heart problems.'

'Well, you'd better get along there, then, hadn't you?'

'Me?' Adele looked startled. 'But Penny asked for you.'

'I was under the impression that you were attending to my patients this morning.' His reply was calm, unruffled.

'Well, yes, but—'

'You'd better hurry up—you don't want a fatality on your hands, do you?'

'Heavens, no!' Adele leapt to her feet and without a backward glance hurried from the room, leaving Casey stretched out in his chair with his hands linked behind his head as if he hadn't a care in the world.

She dashed through Reception, ignoring the startled glances of the receptionists behind the desk, past the waiting room then down the passage to one of the surgery's two treatment rooms where the nurses held their clinics. Not even pausing to knock, she flung open the door and hurried inside, letting the door swing shut behind her.

A woman was lying on the examination couch and Penny was checking her blood pressure. Penny's anxious gaze met Adele's then flickered past her towards the door.

'Where's Casey?' Penny demanded.

'He said for me to assess—'

Penny drew in her breath. 'I'm not happy,' she muttered. 'Her ECG gave cause for concern and now her blood pressure is dropping.'

Adele looked down at the woman on the couch who was about fifty years of age. Her appearance was pale, her breathing shallow and she appeared to have slipped into unconsciousness. 'I'll draw up an injection,' she said. Turning away to the drug cupboards, she began taking out packs containing a syringe and drugs for heart stimulation but before she had the chance to even open the packs there was an urgent shout from Penny.

'She's arrested!'

'The defib?'

'It's in the other treatment room,' said Penny. 'I'll press the alarm button and someone will bring it.'

'There's no sign of a pulse,' said Adele as she checked that the woman was lying flat and that her airway was clear. 'We'll start resuscitation.'

Penny placed a gauze square over the patient's mouth and Adele dragged a footstool to the side of the couch in order to give herself the necessary space to start heart massage. Together they commenced the resuscitation routine—Adele with her hands linked administering five thumps to the patient's chest followed by a short sharp breath into her mouth from Penny, then five more thumps and another breath and so on.

For a moment it was as if Adele had been transported back to her days as a junior doctor in Casualty where this routine had been something of a common occurrence on victims of road accidents who were brought in.

While they were pausing to check for a pulse the door was flung open and Mary appeared with the mobile defibrillator, closely followed by Casey who must have heard the alarm bell and decided to investigate after all.

'There's nothing,' said Penny.

'Keep going,' instructed Adele.

'The defib?'

'While they're setting it up.'

They resumed the mouth-to-mouth resuscitation and the heart massage while Mary and Casey set up the defibrillator, then Casey moved forward with the pads.

'Anything?' he asked, and they all paused again.

'Nothing.' Adele shook her head and then, suddenly mindful that she was only the trainee, stepped from the stool in order to let Casey take over. He, however, calmly passed her the pads. Her gaze flew to his face but his expression was implacable. She was vaguely aware of a look of surprise on Penny's face as if she, too, had assumed that Casey as the senior member of staff present would automatically take over.

Gripping the pads tightly, Adele took a deep breath. 'Stand clear!' she ordered, and as the others stood back she applied the pads, producing the required shock.

The patient's body jumped and arched then Casey checked for a response. 'No,' he said, shaking his head. 'Nothing. Try again.'

Rapidly Adele repeated the procedure—the command

and the application, followed by the moment of anticipation—and this time there was no disappointment for Casey said, 'We have a pulse. Welcome back, Marion.' Gently he smoothed his patient's forehead, brushing her hair from her eyes.

Amidst sighs of relief from Adele, Penny and Mary, Casey looked round at each of them. 'Well done,' he said quietly. 'Thankfully we don't need that procedure here very often but when we do it's nice to know it works so efficiently. I take it...' he glanced at Mary '...there's also an ambulance on the way?'

Mary nodded. 'Yes, Lizzie phoned for one as soon as we heard the alarm bell.'

Casey looked down at Marion again. 'We're going to get you into hospital, Marion,' he said gently as her eyes opened and she looked up at him in bewilderment.

'Hospital...?' she murmured.

'Yes, a little spell in the coronary care unit,' Casey replied. 'You had a cardiac arrest, Marion. Your heart stopped beating but fortunately Dr Brooks and Sister Rudge were on hand to make sure that normal service was resumed.'

'We've let your husband know, Marion,' said Mary. 'Cheryl phoned him at work and he's on his way here.'

'So there you are, Marion, you've nothing to worry about,' said Casey. 'All you have to do is to rest and let others wait on you for a while.'

The ambulance arrived a few minutes later and while Adele was giving details of Marion's treatment and medical condition to the paramedics, Brian Kendry arrived and was shown straight into the treatment room by Lizzie.

After Marion had been taken to hospital, with her husband following the ambulance in his car, Casey was called away to Frances Drew's office to sign a batch of referrals and Adele found herself alone with Penny.

'Well, that was a drama I could have done without on a Monday morning,' said Penny as she set about clearing up.

'It seems to have been all high drama in the last couple of days,' said Adele. She spoke without thinking then immediately wished she'd been more careful as Penny looked up from the couch where she was collecting up the paper sheeting.

'Did Casey get called out to certify that girl's death yesterday? It's all right,' she added, catching sight of Adele's expression. 'I heard it on the news this morning.'

Adele nodded. 'Yes, he did.'

'Was that where you went with him?' Penny's brown eyes narrowed slightly.

'Yes, he asked me to. It…it was pretty harrowing,' she added.

'I dare say it was.' Penny was silent for a moment then she said, 'I'm rather surprised that Casey asked you to go. He's an old hand at that sort of thing but, let's face it, it's all new to you and something like that…well…'

'I have to get used to things like that,' said Adele. 'Especially if I want to be involved in police work. And, after all, I am a doctor.'

'I know.' Penny nodded. 'But you have to admit that yesterday wasn't your usual run-of-the-mill street brawl or pub punch-up, was it?'

'No, it wasn't,' Adele agreed. 'It was pretty ghastly if you must know,' she added after a moment.

'Did it affect you badly?' Penny looked up.

'Yes, it did, actually,' she admitted. 'I'm ashamed to say I needed a brandy afterwards to steady my nerves.'

'Nothing to be ashamed of in that,' said Penny. 'I would probably have needed a couple if it had been me.'

'Apart from the horror of it all and the sadness of that poor girl's death in such a manner and in such a desolate, lonely place, it was also all the implications behind it that made me feel so bad.'

'How do you mean?' Penny tore a length of paper from a large roll and placed it on the couch.

'Well, for a moment there she reminded me of my niece,' said Adele slowly, 'and from that it's only a short leap of imagination to thinking that it could have actually been her. And then I got to thinking of the girl's family and how they must be feeling as they try to come to terms with it all.'

'I know.' Penny gave a little shudder. 'It hardly bears thinking about.'

They were silent for a moment then Adele looked round the treatment room. 'This won't do,' she said. 'I suppose I'd better go and get on.'

'Have you finished surgery?' asked Penny.

'Yes, I'd just seen the last one when you phoned through, but I've no doubt Casey has something else lined up for me—either some house calls or helping him tackle the ever-growing mountain of paperwork.'

'Not working you too hard, is he?' asked Penny casually.

By this time Adele had started walking towards the door but she paused and looked over her shoulder. 'Not really,' she said with a little laugh.

'I hope he bought you the brandy.'

'I'm sorry…?'

'You said you were in need of a brandy last evening— I hope it was Casey who bought it for you.'

'Er, well, yes…sort of.' Suddenly she didn't know quite

what to say. Penny quite obviously thought they had gone to a pub on the way home but if she allowed her to go on thinking that and Penny then mentioned it to Casey who would deny it, she would be made to look very silly. On the other hand, she wasn't too sure she wanted Penny knowing that she had gone to Casey's flat to drink brandy and she certainly didn't want her knowing what else had taken place.

'What do you mean, "sort of"?' Penny wrinkled her nose. 'Either he did or he didn't.'

'Well, we didn't go to the pub,' said Adele. Taking a deep breath and deciding there was nothing else for it, she said, 'He gave me a brandy when we got back here.'

'Really?' Penny had turned away so Adele couldn't see her expression. 'Well, I suppose that was something.'

'Yes, quite.' Adele went then, suddenly unable to cope with any more of that particular conversation. The last thing she wanted was for Penny to think that she was trying to come between her and Casey, but as she left the treatment room she had the feeling that that was exactly what was starting to happen.

CHAPTER EIGHT

DURING the next few days Adele found herself increasingly on edge whenever she was in Casey's company. Whenever she knew she was going to see him, either to do a surgery together or to go on house calls, a kind of anxious tension would set in, followed by anticipation that seemed to build and build until it reached overwhelming proportions.

She was at a loss to explain why this should be—she only knew it had something to do with what had happened between them the night of the police call. She wasn't even sure why. Maybe it was quite simply because what had happened shouldn't have happened and the forbidden element carried an added edge of excitement, but somehow she doubted it was only that. Deep down she knew it had more to do with how she had felt that night, how she had responded to Casey and of how little it had had in common with the way she'd felt about Nigel.

Towards the end of the week Casey told her he felt she was ready to take her own surgeries.

'You'll be fine,' he reassured her, catching sight of her dubious expression. 'And don't forget, at least to start with you'll simply be taking extra surgeries which in theory should only consist of acute situations, urgent things that have just happened that need immediate treatment and can't wait for an appointment.'

'But we all know that isn't always the case,' she observed dryly. 'There will always be the patient who uses the emergency surgery for an update or a second opinion on a chronic situation…'

'True,' Casey agreed, 'and likewise there will be the patient who has put up with a condition for a long time then suddenly snaps and can't bear it a moment longer. Don't forget, you always have options in these situations. If, for example, you don't feel able to deal with something that's more complex than it first appears, you can give temporary relief and ensure that the patient returns to see his or her own GP at a later date.'

'What about referrals?'

'You can, of course, make referrals or if you wish you could leave a memo to the patient's GP about the condition, leaving them to make the decision. You'll find you'll be authorising tests all the time—blood, urine, liver function, thyroid function and so on. In these situations, again it would be courteous to leave a note for the GP concerned, bringing them up to date with what's happening with their patient.'

They had been talking in the treatment room at the end of a cervical smear clinic, and as Casey finished Adele posed the question that had intrigued her since coming to Woolverton House. 'Where will I take these extra surgeries?' she asked, knowing full well there was no spare consulting room.

'Good point.' Casey nodded. Out of the corner of her eye Adele was aware that Penny had come into the treatment room. 'The only spare rooms in the house are the rooms that are used as storerooms and neither of them is suitable at the present time so we've agreed that as one of the partners is off duty on a different day of the week, theirs should be the room you use. Does that sound all right to you?'

'I suppose so.' Adele wrinkled her nose. 'I shall feel like a bit of a nomad but I guess it can't be helped.'

Penny, who had obviously come in on the conversation and had overheard, suddenly spoke. 'What would happen here, Casey, if you took on another partner?'

'As I wanted to do in the first place, you mean?' he asked, looking over his shoulder at Penny.

'Yes, that's right,' she agreed, leaving Adele to believe that she and Casey had discussed the situation at length, probably before her arrival. It suddenly made her feel vulnerable and uneasy.

'Well, I imagine one of the storerooms would be converted,' said Casey. 'Failing that, I guess we might look at planning permission to build on, but I foresee problems there, with this being a listed building. Anyway, that would all be for discussion in the future, but that's the situation at the moment. I've just told Adele, Penny, that I feel she's ready to start taking her own surgeries.'

'Well, that's great.' Penny smiled. 'It'll certainly ease the appointment situation—the reception staff will be delighted,' she added. As Casey began to move towards the door, she said quickly, 'Oh, Casey, don't run away. Could I have a quick word, please?'

'All right, but it'll have to be quick.' Casey looked at his watch. 'I have house calls then a surgery.'

'I know.' Penny moved closer to show him some notes, and as she looked up into his face Adele slipped unnoticed out of the treatment room, leaving the two of them together.

She still found it extremely difficult thinking of Casey and Penny as an item, maybe because there seemed to be so little evidence of it. Knowing Casey as she now did, Adele could imagine him being quite firm about them keeping their relationship very low-key while they were at work, but more strange was that there seemed no sign of very much happening away from work either. But Adele put that down to the fact that perhaps she'd simply not been around at the appropriate times and hadn't seen the pair of them together.

No doubt, she thought as she made her way back to Reception after leaving the treatment room, Penny would seize this opportunity to speak to Casey alone. Suddenly she found herself envying Penny, wishing that she could again talk intimately to Casey as they had done briefly before. She'd been interested in hearing about his family and his background and longed to know more, just as she'd found herself wanting to tell him about her own family and even about her failed relationship with Nigel. For a moment her envy of Penny threatened to spiral out of control as she imagined her and Casey sharing not only intimate details of their families and friends but also every other aspect of their lives, from meals and outings together to possibly holidays, and…sex. Of course, sex. She couldn't imagine Casey being in a relationship and sex not playing an important part. There was something so masculine and intensely virile about him… She shivered slightly, goose-bumps standing up on her skin as she recalled that moment he'd pulled her into his arms. There had been an urgency about it—a sort of raw passion. But she had to stop thinking like this. Casey wasn't hers and was never likely to be. Not, of course, that she even wanted him to be… Did she?

Of course she didn't, she told herself firmly as she walked into the chaotic mass of people that thronged Reception.

At the end of that week was the dinner party to be held by Edward and Celia.

'What will you wear?' asked Cheryl as Adele returned

a batch of notes to Reception after the final surgery.

'I've bought a new top,' Adele replied. 'I thought I could wear it with my black evening trousers.'

'What colour is it?' asked Cheryl, leaning over the reception desk.

'A sort of burnt orange,' said Adele.

'That'll look nice with your colouring,' Lizzie chipped in. 'I've got a new top I'm wearing tonight as well.'

'Are you going to the dinner party?' Adele asked in surprise. She had understood it was only to be for the doctors but maybe she'd been wrong. A peal of laughter from Cheryl soon clarified the position, however.

'Us? To one of Celia Fletcher's dinner parties? You've got to be joking!'

'I just wondered, that's all,' said Adele weakly, then with a surreptitious little glance over her shoulder, she said, 'Why, what's wrong with them?'

'Oh, I'm not saying there's anything wrong with them exactly,' said Cheryl. 'Although, having said that, I can think of better ways of spending a Friday night...'

'Too true,' muttered Lizzie.

'No, it isn't that.' Cheryl flashed a grin at Lizzie. 'It's just that we wouldn't be invited in the first place.'

'Oh.' Adele frowned then asked, 'Isn't there any socialising between the partners and the rest of the staff?'

'Not really.' Cheryl shrugged and shook her head. 'They take us out for a meal at Christmas but that's about it. We girls go out together from time to time—you know, for an Indian or a Chinese or something like that.'

'I think that's a shame,' said Adele slowly. 'I think there should be more social contact. There were masses of social events at the hospital where I worked.'

'Adele's right.' Mary stood up from behind the computer where she had been sitting and from where she had obviously heard every word. 'I think I'll organise something—maybe a cheese and wine party would be nice. I'll see what Rachel thinks.' With that she bustled away towards the practice manager's office.

'Now see what you've done,' groaned Lizzie.

'Sorry!' Adele chuckled, turning as Toby came out of his consulting room.

'Have I missed a joke?' he asked, blinking and looking round.

'Not really. We were just talking about socialising and about tonight's dinner party,' said Adele.

'Oh, Lord, yes,' said Toby. 'I'd forgotten about that for a while.'

'Sounds like you're not too keen on going,' said Adele quietly as she fell into step beside him and they began to make their way out of the front of the building and round to the courtyard and the entrance to the flats.

'Oh, it'll be all right when we get there,' said Toby. 'It's one of those things it's difficult to drum up any enthusiasm over, but I have to say Celia really does go to a lot of trouble and she's an excellent cook—the food is always superb at these dos.'

'Do they have many of them?' asked Adele curiously as they began to climb the stairs.

'A couple or so a year,' Toby replied. 'I gather this one is in your honour.'

'So I believe.' Adele nodded. By this time they had reached the first-floor landing where Toby paused for a moment. 'Would you like a lift there?' he asked.

'That's kind of you,' said Adele. 'But I can take my car.'

'Wouldn't hear of it,' said Toby. 'Can't have the guest

of honour unable to have a drink. I'll meet you down here…what, about seven?'

'Yes, all right, thanks, Toby.'

Adele found herself getting ready with extra care that evening, taking more trouble than usual over her make-up, hair and nails. When she had finished she carefully stepped into the pair of black crêpe trousers she had bought in Chester, and which had cost her nearly a week's wages, but when she went to put on the new top she had told the girls about she was unable to find it. She had only bought it a few days previously in one of the local high street shops especially to wear at the dinner party. She searched her wardrobe and the chest of drawers, and even went through the rubbish bag, fearing it may have got caught up with things she had thrown away, but there was no sign of it. In the end, in desperation she took from the wardrobe a gold sleeveless top with a roll neck, and by the time she had pulled it over her head and rearranged her hair it was time for her to meet Toby.

He was waiting for her on the landing looking somehow very boyish in evening dress, almost like a student going to a freshers' ball. He had obviously just washed his hair, which still flopped across his forehead and over his glasses. 'You look nice,' he said admiringly as together they made their way down to the courtyard.

'Thank you.' Adele smiled. 'You don't look so bad yourself.' She was amused to see the colour touch his cheeks as if he wasn't used to compliments.

'I was going to ask Casey if he wanted to come with us,' he said as he opened the passenger door of his car for Adele, 'but there was no reply when I knocked on his door. Either he's already left or he's been called out. Knowing Casey, anything's possible.' He started the engine and they drew out of the courtyard onto the high street. 'Have you been to the Fletchers' home?' he asked as he joined the flow of traffic.

'No.' Adele shook her head. 'Do they live far away?'

'About a mile and a half. It's west of the town up at Jacob's Rise. It's an exclusive area that has been developed in the last ten years or so. As you'll see, there are some pretty impressive properties up there.'

'What's Celia like?' asked Adele after a moment.

'Celia?' Toby gave a rare chuckle. 'Oh, she's all right really, I suppose. But she does have the tendency to want to organise things which, I guess, is fine to a point, but unfortunately she includes other people's lives in that as well. She's notorious as a matchmaker,' he said, throwing Adele a sidelong glance. 'To be honest with you, I've been dreading tonight,' he admitted, 'because I'm sure she'll have someone lined up for me. On the other hand, I dare say she may have given up on me by now. She must think I'm a dead loss.'

'I'm sure that isn't true,' protested Adele. Casting him a sidelong glance she said, 'But would she do that? Have someone lined up, I mean?'

'She's done it before,' Toby replied darkly. 'The last one she lined up for me was impossible. I felt obliged to take her home and she kept ringing me for weeks afterwards.'

'Oh, poor old you,' said Adele sympathetically. 'What a nightmare! I say,' she added in sudden alarm, 'I hope she hasn't lined anyone up for me.'

'I expect you'll escape this time as she hasn't yet met you,' said Toby solemnly, 'but be warned for the future.'

'The answer, I suppose,' said Adele thoughtfully 'is to ask if you can bring someone along or, failing that, to at least say that you're seeing someone even if you aren't.'

'I was going to do that tonight,' admitted Toby sheepishly. 'I was going to ask Penny then if…if she agreed I would have checked it out with Celia. But, then, I don't know, I chickened out.'

'Penny?' Adele turned to him. The surprise in her voice must have been obvious.

'I know, pathetic, isn't it?' Toby must have thought her surprise was over his lack of courage rather than his choice of partner. 'I'm afraid I'm always chickening out over things like that.'

'No,' said Adele quickly, 'I didn't mean that. I was surprised that you were thinking of asking Penny, because of Casey. After all, she wouldn't want anyone to think that you and she—'

'What about Casey?' Toby cut her short. He threw her a startled glance, taking his eyes from the road then, as the car swerved slightly to the left, being forced to concentrate again.

'Well, they're an item,' said Adele weakly.

'Are they? I didn't know that.' Toby looked shattered, leaving Adele in no doubt that he hadn't only been wanting Penny as an escort to fend off Celia's matchmaking. Suddenly she felt guilty at being the one to impart news that had obviously had such an impact. He risked another glance in her direction. 'How did *you* know?' he asked.

'Penny herself told me,' said Adele. 'The day I arrived. She said she and Casey were an item, that it was early days but that she was very hopeful.'

'Good heavens!' said Toby. 'I had no idea.' He paused, as if allowing the news to sink in, then he said, 'Well, I have to say Casey's a dark horse—he's said nothing.'

'I know,' said Adele. 'I thought that, then I came to the conclusion that it was probably because he didn't want a lot of gossip and speculation amongst the staff.'

'Yes,' agreed Toby miserably. 'I dare say.'

They travelled on in silence for a while, each apparently lost in their own thoughts. It had been a beautiful day, slightly autumnal but still with the warmth of late summer, and as they climbed the hill out of the town, before them in a spectacular crimson sky the sun was sinking into great banks of gold-edged clouds.

'I'm sorry,' said Adele at last, breaking the silence, 'that I had to be the one to tell you.'

'Don't worry,' said Toby gloomily. 'It's the story of my life. I always leave things until they're too late. It's my own fault. I've been plucking up courage for ages to ask Penny out…' He trailed off with a shrug. 'I had no idea she was seeing anyone else.' He paused then shook his head. 'But Casey,' he went on after a moment, 'that does surprise me. I wouldn't have thought Casey was her type at all. In fact, I would have thought that Casey was perhaps more your type…'

'My type? Oh, no,' she said quickly, 'not me. Besides, I'm off men at the moment. Present company excepted, of course,' she added.

'In that case,' said Toby, suddenly brightening up, 'why don't we pretend we are an item this evening—just to thwart any plans that Celia might have?'

'What an excellent idea,' agreed Adele with a laugh.

They arrived at the Fletchers' residence a few minutes later, only to find that the practice Land Rover was already parked on the drive alongside Edward's Jaguar and Rachel's VW.

'Casey's here,' observed Toby as they climbed out of the car. 'Let's hope if he's come straight from a call-out that he changed first. I wouldn't put it past him to turn up wearing jeans and a sweater.'

'And what would Celia make of that?' murmured Adele

as they approached the house, an imposing mock-Georgian residence.

'He would be forgiven—simply because he's Casey,' Toby reached out and rang the doorbell. 'In Celia's eyes Casey can do no wrong.'

'I have a feeling we could be in for an interesting evening—' Adele began, breaking off as the front door opened.

Edward stood on the threshold, immaculate and distinguished-looking in evening dress but with a drawn tiredness around his eyes that reminded his two young colleagues of his present medical problems. 'Adele! Toby! Come on in.' He stood aside, allowing them both to enter the spacious hallway. As he closed the front door behind them a tall, exquisitely groomed woman came through into the hall. Her blonde, almost white hair was cut into a fashionable, jaw-length bob and she was dressed in a close-fitting, ankle-length black dress. She wore a minimum of jewellery—pearl studs in her ears, a pearl choker at her throat and a single gold bracelet on one of her slim wrists—but the overall effect was stunning. Adele found herself thinking that Celia Fletcher must have been a very beautiful woman in her youth, but as her gaze met that of her hostess she was momentarily puzzled by the expression in her cool grey eyes. If asked, she would have sworn that Celia Fletcher's reaction on seeing her for the first time was one of shock, but later she would question that for it was swiftly replaced by other fleeting expressions—recognition, puzzlement? Adele couldn't be sure, and as the older woman came forward to greet her she even wondered if she might have been mistaken.

'Adele, my dear.' Not waiting for her husband to make the introductions, Celia took Adele's hands in hers. 'How good to meet you at last. I've heard so much about you.'

'It is kind of you to invite me,' said Adele, surprisingly touched by the warmth of the older woman's welcome.

'Toby, hello, how charming you look.' Briefly Celia touched Toby's arm. 'Come into the drawing room. We are all here now except Jeanette. She called to say she was running late but she'll be here shortly.'

As Celia led the way into the drawing room Adele had to fight a sudden overwhelming urge to giggle as Toby suddenly offered her his arm. In order to keep up the pretence they had agreed upon she took it, but as they entered the room all such notions of hilarity flew as she caught sight of Casey. He was standing by a magnificent Adam fireplace, a drink in one hand, talking to Rachel's husband Matt. He must have seen a flicker of interest in Matt's eyes for he turned and looked towards the door, his gaze immediately meeting Adele's as she and Toby entered the room.

She wasn't certain whether it was the sight of that powerful body in a tuxedo or whether it was the expression in his eyes that caused her heart to miss a beat, but, whatever it was, for a moment it threw her and she was glad that Edward caused a diversion by asking Toby and herself what they would like to drink.

But that moment seemed to set the tone for the evening for with every movement, every glance Adele was excruciatingly aware of Casey.

Jeanette eventually arrived, apologising profusely for her lateness, full of stories of a difficult patient and her even more difficult teenage children—her daughter, whom she'd reluctantly allowed to go on a sleep-over at a friend's, and her son, who had just dropped out of his college course in order to hitchhike to Morocco.

'Lord,' said Toby with feeling, 'I don't think I ever want kids.'

'Well, ours are still small,' said Rachel. 'And I have to say we don't seem to have had too much trouble yet.'

'You wait until they leave home,' said Edward darkly. 'That's when your problems really start. At least when they're small you know where they are.'

Gradually they drifted into the dining room, to a table bathed in candlelight, gleaming with silver and cut glass and dotted with ivy leaves and fresh cream rosebuds. Once again Toby was at Adele's side and once again she took his arm, only to find that Celia had almost pre-empted their motives and seated them together.

'Do you think *we* could have been the object of her matchmaking this time?' murmured Adele under cover of them taking their seats.

'Who knows?' Toby murmured in her ear as he eased her into her chair. 'But let's not disappoint her.'

'No, quite.' Adele smiled dazzlingly up into his face, only to find when looking across the table that Casey's gaze was upon her again—and this time there was no mistaking the scowl on his face.

Toby had certainly been quite right when he'd said that Celia went to a lot of trouble when she gave a dinner party. Smoked salmon and goat's cheese preceded succulent rack of lamb with rosemary sauce and tender vegetables, followed by summer pudding and whipped cream.

The conversation around the table ranged from shop talk—everything from staffing problems to the NHS—to some amusing incidents about local characters. Then Celia drew attention to her with a question about her home and family.

'Adele was at a hospital in Chester, weren't you, Adele?' It was Toby who replied. A slightly flushed, unusually animated Toby whose condition must be attributed to the circumstances rather than the mineral water he was drinking.

'Yes,' Adele agreed, 'that's right. I was an SHO.'

'No desire to specialise?' asked Jeanette, leaning forward slightly to peer down the table at Adele.

'For a time maybe,' Adele replied. 'But general practice had long been an ambition, as had police work. Stourborne Abbas has presented an opportunity to combine both.' As she spoke, once again her gaze met Casey's but still his expression was set without so much as a flicker of emotion or amusement, leaving her feeling suddenly rather nervous.

At Celia's suggestion they moved into the drawing room for coffee, with Toby once again taking Adele's arm and cosily seating himself by her side on one of the two vast sofas. And it was while sipping her coffee that Adele realised that Casey wasn't there. Idly she was wondering where he was when suddenly he strode into the room, his mobile phone in one hand.

'Celia,' he said, 'I'm so sorry but I have to go.'

'Oh, no,' said Celia, 'not the police again. Can't they leave you alone for one evening?'

'That's the way it goes, I'm afraid.' He turned and looked at Adele and she suddenly found herself holding her breath. 'I'd like Adele to come with me on this one.'

'Oh, surely not,' protested Celia. 'After all—'

'She has much to learn,' said Casey firmly. 'And this is the only way.'

'I'll come,' said Adele, setting her coffee-cup down and rising to her feet. 'Of course I will.' She turned briefly to her hosts. 'Thank you, Celia, and you, Edward, for a truly delightful evening,' she said, and then she fled, following Casey out of the room.

CHAPTER NINE

'WHAT the hell was all that about?'

They had left the house in silence but no sooner had they climbed into the Land Rover than Casey almost exploded.

Adele, who was more concerned about her expensive black crêpe trousers and what might befall them in the rather dubious interior of the staff vehicle, threw him a startled glance. 'All what?' She frowned, wondering what on earth he meant.

'All that rubbish between you and Toby, that's what!' He positively growled in response and for a moment she still didn't understand to what he was referring. 'He's been drooling all over you like some lovesick puppy since the moment you arrived.'

'Oh, that!' Adele chuckled as at last it dawned on her what he was getting at. 'Actually,' she explained, 'we travelled together—'

'Why did you do that?' Casey demanded as he started the engine and with a squeal of tyres on the loose gravel path drove out onto the main road.

'Well, Toby suggested it…'

'I bet he did.'

'He said as I was the guest of honour it would be nice for me to be able to have a drink,' she carried on, ignoring his interruption and at the same time fastening her seat belt. 'I thought it was very kind of him. Obviously he thought it was silly taking so many cars when we were all going from the same place. He even knocked on your door,' she added, 'to see if you wanted a lift, but you weren't there.'

'That would have cramped his style a bit,' muttered Casey.

'So where were you?' Adele shot him a puzzled glance, wondering just what the reason was for his surly mood.

'I had a police call-out.'

'And you didn't call me?' Adele raised her eyebrows.

'I thought you'd be getting ready,' he said abruptly. 'I was already dressed.'

'Well, yes, actually, I suppose I was getting ready but...but I have to say I feel a bit bad about Toby now.'

'Why? Why should you feel bad?' There was a contemptuous air about Casey now that somehow irritated Adele even further.

'Well, he was good enough to bring me and now...well, now I feel as if I've just dumped him.'

'We can go back if you like.' Casey eased his foot off the accelerator. 'I'll turn around and drop you off.'

'No, of course not,' said Adele hastily. 'I have to go with you now. You made it plain enough to everyone that you felt I should go.'

He didn't answer and after travelling in silence for a while at what seemed to Adele like a speed bordering on the dangerous she said, 'So what is it?'

'What is what?' His voice was tight now, controlled, but his gaze was directed firmly at the road ahead.

'This call-out.' She struggled to keep the impatience out of her tone for increasingly there was something about Casey that night that was downright infuriating. 'Did the police say what it was? Was it anything to do with the first call-out or was it something new?'

'I've no idea,' he replied tightly.

'What do you mean, you've no idea?' She frowned.

'Didn't the police give any idea why they were calling you out? They usually do, don't they?'

'Yes,' he agreed, 'they do. But on this occasion they didn't, mainly, I suppose, because they didn't phone.'

Slowly she turned to look at him but his expression was still fixed, giving away nothing. 'I don't understand,' she said. 'You say the police didn't phone you but back there at the Fletchers', you went out of the room and came back some considerable time later with your phone in your hand, saying you had to go.'

He made no comment, neither agreeing with her nor contradicting her.

'You said it was the police…'

'No,' he interrupted calmly. 'Celia assumed that.'

'But then you said you wanted me to go with you.'

'That's true.' He nodded.

'You led everyone to believe that you thought I should go because it would be of benefit to me.'

'Again that is what they chose to believe.' He shrugged.

'So if there's no police call-out, why did we leave?' asked Adele in bewilderment. Suddenly all this seemed to be getting beyond her—maybe it was something to do with Edward's excellent wine that had been served with dinner.

'Because I'd had enough.' His reply was so terse that for a moment Adele thought she'd misheard him.

'I'm sorry,' she said. 'You'd what?'

'I said it was because I'd had enough. I told you dinner parties quite definitely are not my cup of tea.'

'I know you did but… but…don't you think that was…rude?' She had been about to say outrageous, so flabbergasted was she by his admission, but she changed her mind after another glance at his scowling, uncompromising profile.

'Why was it rude?' he demanded.

'Well…Edward…Celia…they went to a lot of trouble and, well, Edward is your friend, your partner…'

'I know that,' he snapped. 'And in spite of what you might now believe, I am very fond of both of them and just as a matter of interest I don't think what I did was rude at all. If I'd done it in the middle of dinner that may have been different. The meal was long over, everyone had finished their coffee. All that would have happened—all that is happening now—is more gossip, probably more brandy for those fortunate enough not to be driving, and yet more gossip.'

'Well, yes, maybe,' Adele agreed, 'but I still think…well, I mean what made you think I might have had enough? What gave you the right to decide for me?' Suddenly she was angry. Angry at what she had perceived as his apparent rudeness, but even more angry that in his arrogance he should have assumed that she was of the same frame of mind as himself and for including her in his scheme.

'Hadn't you had enough?' He threw her a cynical, side-long glance. 'Go on, be honest.'

'Actually, no, I was enjoying my evening if you must know.'

'You seemed more than willing to come with me when I suggested it,' he replied. 'In fact, I would say "eager" is the word that springs to mind.'

'That was because I thought we were going to a police call,' Adele protested.

'So you feel that would have justified us leaving when we did?' he asked coolly.

'Well, yes, obviously…' She trailed off, still having to struggle to control her temper. 'As it is,' she went on after a moment, 'you've put me in an impossible situation. What will I say if anyone asks me what the police call was about?'

'Who's likely to ask you that?' His lip curled slightly and she couldn't help noticing that his scar stood out more than usual, making him look tougher than ever and somehow even more incongruous in his tuxedo and black tie.

'Well, Edward might...or Jeanette, even Rachel... and...and Toby. Toby is sure to.'

There was another squeal of tyres as Casey slammed on the brakes then reversed the Land Rover for several yards before swinging it into a sharp left turn.

'Where are we going now?' asked Adele in alarm.

'The police station,' snapped Casey. 'Isn't that where you want to go?'

'Well, yes, but...if there isn't anything to go there for...'

'If it'll make you feel less guilty, we'll go there and check on the patient I saw earlier this evening.'

Adele remained silent after that as they hurtled through the night to the police station. She was silent because she couldn't think what else to say with Casey in this strange, almost belligerent mood. As they drew up sharply on the police forecourt and Casey switched off the engine, she threw him a tentative glance. 'This patient...' she began.

He'd been about to climb out of the Land Rover but he paused and looked over his shoulder at her. 'What about him?'

'Don't you think I should know what it's all about—if I'm to go in with you, I mean...'

'He'd been in a fight—usual stuff. Two gangs clashed and our client got bashed over the head with a baseball bat. He's suffered slight concussion but not enough for him to be hospitalised. Is that enough?'

'Yes. I suppose so.' Miserably Adele climbed out of the

vehicle, pulling on her black jacket as she did so. She didn't like Casey being this way with her, so abrupt and offhand, but even more to the point she couldn't think of any reason why he was. He'd been fine at work that day, easygoing and relaxed, even joking with her about taking solo surgeries the following week. And now he was in a really foul mood which, when she really thought about it, seemed to have started at some point during the dinner party. Maybe someone had said something to upset him or maybe it was quite simply that he really did loathe dinner parties, but whatever it was Adele wished it wasn't happening.

She almost had to run to keep up with him as he strode ahead of her into the police station. Alan Munro was behind the desk and he looked up in surprise as they almost erupted into Reception.

'Good grief!' he said. 'If that's not telepathy I don't know what is. I've just phoned for the paramedics.' Disbelievingly he glanced at the telephone receiver in his hand.

'The concussion?' said Casey.

'No, he's fine.' Alan shook his head. 'This is a young girl who was brought in with a crowd of youngsters after neighbours complained of a loud party. These kids were out of their minds on booze and there were no adults present. Since they've been here this particular girl seems to have taken a turn for the worse.'

'We'd better take a look at her, then,' said Casey.

As Alan led them through Reception he glanced back at them both, taking in their attire. 'Been somewhere special?' he asked.

'Dinner party,' Casey muttered.

'Good time?' asked Alan conversationally.

'Yes.' Adele quickly intervened, thinking it was probably better that she should answer that particular question. 'Yes, very good, thanks.'

They were led into a room where a WPC was supervising two teenage girls. One was curled up on a bunk and the other was vomiting into a bucket.

'Some of the parents have been to collect their offspring,' said Alan. 'But we haven't even managed to get names out of these two. We suspect they are both minors so we've called the social worker. But this is the one we've been the most concerned about.' He indicated the girl on the bunk who had her back to the door and who was partly covered by a grey blanket.

Casey had stopped briefly beside the girl with her head in the bucket, and it was Adele who crouched beside the bunk and gently lifted back the blanket. 'Hello,' she said gently. 'Can you tell me your name?'

At first there was no movement from the girl then with a low moan she turned onto her back, flinging one arm above her head, and in the harsh overhead lighting Adele saw her face. It was deathly pale, her eyes circled with kohl, lashes matted with mascara, while her black hair was tangled. She was an absolute mess, but none of this prevented Adele from recognising her from the time she had come into the surgery during the previous week to wait for her mother after missing her school bus.

'Casey.' Adele looked over her shoulder and as Casey looked up, she said, 'It's Jeanette's daughter, Lara. And yes, she is a minor,' she added to the police sergeant. 'She's only fourteen and her name is Lara Maynard.'

With a muttered exclamation Casey moved across the cell and crouched down beside her, taking the girl's wrist as he did so. 'She's very dehydrated,' he said after a moment. Looking across at the other girl, he said, 'Has Lara been taking anything other than alcohol?'

The girl, her damp blonde hair hanging over her face and around her shoulders, looked up.

'We have to know,' Casey added urgently.

'Ecstasy,' muttered the girl. 'Only one,' she added defiantly.

'And you,' he said. 'Have you taken any?'

'Yeah, the same,' she said, before retching helplessly again into the bucket.

'This is exactly what I suspected,' said Alan grimly. 'The ambulance should be here shortly.'

'I'll get my bag,' said Casey. 'I want to put a drip up right away.'

'Shall I get it for you?' asked Adele.

'No,' said Casey briefly. 'I want you to phone Jeanette and tell her what's happening.'

Adele's heart sank. How did you phone a woman, a colleague and friend at that, and tell her that her fourteen-year-old daughter was in police custody and about to be transported to hospital suffering from the effects of drugs and alcohol? But it had to be done. Taking her mobile phone from her pocket, she decided first to try the Fletchers' and see if Jeanette was still there. Celia answered the phone.

'Celia, it's Adele. I'm so sorry to bother you but is Jeanette still with you?'

'Yes, she's here. I'll fetch her for you.' Celia paused. 'Is there anything wrong, Adele?'

'I think I'd better speak to Jeanette,' she replied.

'Very well. Hold on.'

A minute later Jeanette came to the phone. 'Adele?' she said.

'Jeanette, I'm sorry but there's no easy way to say this. We're at the police station. I'm afraid your daughter, Lara, is here—'

'Lara? She can't be, she's sleeping over at a friend's house…'

'It appears there was a complaint about a loud party going on,' Adele continued. 'The police were called and several of the youngsters were brought into the station.'

'So are they in trouble?' demanded Jeanette. She sighed crossly. 'I'd better come down there.'

'Actually, Jeanette, I think there's rather more to it than that.'

'What do you mean?' There was real alarm in Jeanette's voice now.

'Well, they had all been drinking and…some had been taking drugs.'

'Drugs? Oh, my God! But listen, Lara wouldn't have taken drugs. She knows all the dangers—I've drummed it into her often enough.'

'I'm sorry, Jeanette,' said Adele gently. 'But I'm afraid she has. Casey is worried about her—there's an ambulance on the way…'

'I'll go straight to A and E,' said Jeanette. She was suddenly in professional mode—the anguish of parenthood for the time being put aside.

'Have you got anyone to go with you?' asked Adele.

'Yes, my son Nick is at home. I'll phone him.' Jeanette hung up then and Adele made her way back to the cell where she found Casey in the process of setting up an infusion after inserting a cannula in the back of Lara's hand.

The other girl, whose name turned out to be Chloe, had stopped retching and was sitting on a chair with her head in her hands, watched by the WPC.

'Are you feeling any better?' Adele crouched down in front of her.

'No.' The girl shook her head. 'I feel terrible.'

'So where were you?' asked Adele gently.

'We went to a party at the house of a boy from school. My dad thought I was on a sleep-over at Lara's house—he's going to kill us.'

'Only if he gets there before Lara's mother,' said Casey dryly. Looking up at Adele, he said, 'Did you get hold of Jeanette?'

'Yes, she was still at the Fletchers'. I told her what was happening. She's going straight to the hospital.'

'Good idea. Was anyone going with her?'

'Her son, I believe.' Adele looked down at Lara who now had her eyes closed and was lying very still. 'How is she?' she said.

'She's unconscious.' Casey shook his head. At that moment there were sounds of activity in the corridor outside the cell and a second later Alan opened the door and admitted the paramedics.

Lara was immediately given oxygen to assist her breathing and the paramedics took her to the waiting ambulance. Casey went with them while Adele stayed with Chloe, and when the paramedics returned for Chloe, Adele accompanied them out of the police station.

Casey was in the back of the ambulance, still attending to Lara, checking her pulse, blood pressure and breathing, but once Chloe was settled on the opposite couch to Lara he looked at the attendant paramedic. 'They're all yours,' he said.

Jumping from the back of the ambulance, he stood alongside Adele and Alan as the WPC climbed into the ambulance and the driver closed the doors.

A couple of minutes later the ambulance swept out of the police forecourt with its blue light flashing, and the three of them made their way back into the station.

'So that was Dr Maynard's daughter?' said Alan. 'Do you think she'll be OK?'

'Hard to say at this stage,' said Casey grimly. 'Her heartbeat was very erratic. The worrying part is that even those who get through this acute phase can sometimes be left with brain damage.'

'Why do they do it?' Sadly Alan shook his head then, looking from Casey to Adele, he said, 'Well, I think that just about winds things up for the time being. Bit of luck, you coming in like that when you did.'

'Yes, quite.' Casey nodded but he didn't look at Adele. 'But now we're here,' he added, 'it won't do any harm to look at the concussion case again.'

'As you wish.' Alan nodded and led the way once again back to the cells.

They left the station a little later after Casey had checked that his concussion patient was indeed all right. In silence they climbed into the Land Rover, and as Casey put his key into the ignition Adele spoke. 'I felt sorry for Jeanette,' she said.

'She's certainly got her hands full with those offspring of hers,' Casey agreed.

'What happened to her husband?'

'They separated years ago then divorced. I don't think he's played much of a part in his children's upbringing.'

'It can't be easy, bringing up children in today's climate,' said Adele slowly. 'And it seems to me it doesn't make much difference whether they are brought up in an environment like the Procters' or in the supposedly privileged background of a doctor's home.'

'I'm sure you're right.' Casey paused then, drawing out onto the main road, he said, 'How did Jeanette take it?'

'She was shocked, I think, naturally—after all, she thought her daughter was simply at a sleep-over at a friend's house. It must have been pretty shattering to hear where she'd ended up. I only hope her son will be more supportive. Didn't she say he'd dropped out of his college course?'

'Apparently, yes.' Casey nodded. 'At least Celia knows we were at the police station,' he said dryly. After a pause and with a touch of curiosity in his voice he said, 'What did you think of Celia?'

Adele considered for a moment. 'Charming,' she said at last, 'very elegant, but, I have to say there was something in the way she greeted me that left me wondering.'

'What do you mean?' In the darkness of the vehicle's interior Adele knew he was frowning.

'She looked startled. I almost felt that she thought she recognised me—but it couldn't have been that because we certainly haven't met before.' She paused. 'Have you known her for long?'

Casey didn't reply immediately, instead concentrating on negotiating a traffic roundabout. As the Land Rover gathered sped once more on a straight stretch of road, he said, 'Celia and I go back a long way.'

'Really?' Adele was faintly surprised and at the same time intrigued. There must, after all, be a twenty-year age difference between Celia Fletcher and Casey, which surely ruled out any sort of romantic attachment. But on the other hand, with Casey, who knew? With his chequered past anything was possible.

'We worked at the same hospital,' he said. 'I was doing my training and Celia was secretary to one of the consultants.'

'Was she married to Edward then?'

'Oh, yes. She had returned to work after her family had grown up.'

'And what about now—does she still work now?'

Casey shook his head. 'No, she retired when they moved here to Stourborne Abbas and Edward founded the practice. It's Celia whom I have to thank for me being here. It was her who suggested to Edward that he contact me as a prospective partner.' He paused. 'Celia has a knack for that sort of thing—fitting a person into the right situation.'

'Toby said something like that, too,' said Adele wryly.

'What do you mean?' That irritable edge was back in Casey's tone—the one that had been there earlier when they'd first left the Fletchers' home.

'Toby wasn't quite so polite about it as you—he said Celia was too fond of organising other people's lives.'

'I suppose some might see it that way,' replied Casey tightly.

'He also said she was very fond of matchmaking. Apparently, once in the past she lined up some dreadful woman for Toby who clung to him like a limpet and who continued to pester him for ages afterwards. I'm afraid it's made him very wary of Celia's dinner parties.'

'He didn't seem to have any such worries tonight.' Casey spoke in the same clipped tone. 'He was all over you like a rash.'

'He wasn't!' protested Adele.

'Well, it certainly looked that way from where I was sitting,' muttered Casey, 'and I'm sure it didn't go unnoticed by the others either.'

'Oh, heavens! Do you really think so?' Adele stared at him in dismay. 'I'll have to tell Toby he overdid it.'

There was silence for a moment then slowly Casey said, 'What do you mean, tell him he overdid it?'

'Well, we arranged it.' In the darkness Adele turned to look at him. 'We decided rather than risk Celia having lined anyone up for us we would pretend we were an item.' In the sudden silence Adele heard Casey sharply draw in his breath. 'As it happened,' she went on, 'we gradually came to the conclusion that she had lined us up for each other anyway…'

'So you aren't an item?' He almost barked the question, making Adele jump.

'Well, no. No, of course not.' She paused and looked at him again but he was staring straight ahead as by this time they had turned into the high street and he was preparing to enter the courtyard of Woolverton House. 'Surely,' she said incredulously, 'you didn't think that?'

Casey brought the vehicle to a halt and switched off the engine. 'I didn't know quite what to think,' he growled.

'But I'd told you that I'm not into relationships at the moment.'

'I know,' he said abruptly. 'I suppose that was why I was surprised by tonight's performance.'

They were silent for a while then in a small voice, Adele said, 'I guess I'd better tell Toby that we came across as a little too convincing.'

'Yes, maybe you had, if you don't want staff gossip and speculation,' Casey agreed tersely. 'If it fooled me it will have fooled others and there's a good chance that it might have given Toby himself a few ideas.'

Adele wanted to tell him that he was wrong on that score, that Toby certainly wasn't interested in her, that it was Penny he wanted—but how could she when it was Casey himself who was involved with Penny? She could just imagine the ensuing scene. Casey's reaction to the little subterfuge between herself and Toby had been bad enough, let alone what it would be like if he thought Toby was interested in Penny. She shuddered at the thought as she stepped down from the Land Rover. She would have walked straight round and entered the house but found Casey barring her way.

'Casey…?' she looked up at him.

'Adele…' he murmured.

There was something about the sound of her name on his lips that was almost Adele's undoing, and in spite of all her previous resolutions she suddenly wanted him to take her in his arms again the way he had before. She wanted everyone else to go away—Penny, Nigel, Toby, everyone—leaving just herself and Casey here in the darkness, safe in a world of their own. And for a moment it would seem that theirs was but a single thought and of mutual intent for he took a step closer and held out his hand.

There was no telling what would have happened next for there was a slight movement behind them and Penny herself suddenly appeared out of the shadows of the doorway.

'Hello,' she said, her eyes on Casey. 'I wondered where you had got to. Toby was back ages ago. He said you'd had a call-out and that Jeanette's daughter was involved. I wondered what it was all about.'

Leaving Casey to explain, Adele fled into the house and up the stairs to her flat, suddenly unable to cope with anything else that night.

CHAPTER TEN

EXHAUSTED from the evening's events both physically and mentally, Adele fell asleep almost as soon as her head touched the pillow but her dreams were troubled and she awoke suddenly to find it was only three o'clock and she'd slept for barely two hours. Turning over, she attempted to go back to sleep but was so wide awake she knew sleep was now going to be impossible.

Slipping out of bed, she padded to the kitchen, poured a glass of milk and took it back to bed where she sat for a long time going over the events of the evening. If she was honest, the aspect that had intrigued and puzzled her had been Casey's mood, which from the moment she and Toby had arrived at the dinner party had been less than friendly and which as the evening had progressed had grown into something bordering on hostile. She'd been annoyed when he'd used the pretext of a police call-out as an excuse to get not only himself but her as well away from the party and then later he'd admitted he'd assumed that her and Toby's pretence at togetherness had been genuine.

So had that been the reason for his surly behaviour? It had certainly seemed that way. In fact, if she hadn't known better she would have said that he'd seemed jealous by the attention that she and Toby had been paying each other. But that was ridiculous—why would he be jealous? Irritated maybe, in view of her having told him that she wasn't ready for another relationship, although even that didn't give him the right to question her actions, but cer-

tainly not jealous. After all, he had Penny so why would
he be jealous of someone paying her, Adele, some attention?

The only reason for that would be if he had feelings for
her himself and surely there wasn't the remotest possibility
of that. Was there?

Adele shifted her position, disturbed even by the
thought. They had shared those intimate moments in his
flat, it was true, but surely that had been no more than him
comforting her after the traumatic nature of the case they
had just attended. Then again that very night there had
been that moment when there had been no telling what
might have happened if Penny hadn't appeared. But the
fact was, Penny *had* appeared and she was the woman in
Casey's life.

But, a perverse little voice persisted at the back of her
mind, supposing there was no woman in his life, supposing
Casey and Penny weren't an item and he was free, what
then? How would she feel if he wanted to start a relationship with her? She had been adamant that she wanted no
involvement with anyone—that it was too soon following
her break-up with Nigel, but that had been then, before
she'd got to know Casey. What about now? Did it make
a difference now that Casey had come into her life?

Somewhere deep inside she felt a quick, fierce throb of
desire. There was something intensely exciting about the
idea of herself and Casey being together. Then deliberately
she tried to dismiss the thought. It would never happen.
For a start Casey was her trainer and she couldn't imagine
that Edward or the other partners would look upon any
such relationship kindly and even if they did, there was
still Penny.

It always came back to Penny. Deliberately Adele set
her empty glass down on her bedside table. Penny had

shown her nothing but kindness ever since her arrival and she knew she could never do anything to hurt her.

All she could do in the future, she told herself firmly, was to keep Casey at arm's length, especially if he was weak enough to believe that he could have her while he was with Penny. Was that his intention? She'd been down that road before with Nigel and it had led to nothing but heartbreak—she certainly didn't intend letting it happen again.

In this new, resolute frame of mind she finally settled down again and attempted to go back to sleep, but just as she was on the point of dropping off an image of Penny and Casey in bed together—which, no doubt, they were—came into her mind. It tormented her so much that it was another hour before finally she slept.

It had already been decided that Adele should start taking surgeries on her own the following week. From her point of view it couldn't have come at a better time for it would mean that she and Casey would see much less of each other. She would, of course, still be expected to report to him on a routine daily basis or if any matter arose that was beyond her capabilities, but the main part of her days would be spent alone, dealing with extra surgeries and home visits for whichever of the partners was off duty.

When she arrived in Reception in readiness for her first solo surgery on Monday morning she wasn't surprised to find the whole place abuzz with speculation about Jeanette's family troubles.

'You were there, weren't you?' demanded Lizzie when she caught sight of Adele. 'At the police station?'

'Yes,' Adele admitted guardedly. 'I was.'

'What did Lara look like?'

'I should say a reason to put anyone off experimenting with drugs,' Adele replied firmly.

'It's Dr Maynard I feel sorry for,' said Cheryl. 'She's had nothing but worry from those kids of hers—ungrateful little devils.'

'That's enough,' Mary intervened. 'We have work to do. Dr Brooks, needless to say, Dr Maynard isn't in this morning so if you would like to take surgery in her room.'

'Of course.' Adele nodded. 'Have we heard how Lara is by the way?'

Mary nodded. 'Yes, Rachel phoned the hospital and they said she's stable and comfortable.'

'Well, I guess that's something,' said Adele with a sigh. She knew she would carry in her mind for some considerable time the image of Lara lying in the police cell with her ashen face and her eyes rolling.

'At least she's alive,' said Lizzie. 'I heard on the news this morning that the police in Bath have arrested someone for the murder of that girl.'

'I bet it was the mother's boyfriend,' said Cheryl. 'He looked a nasty piece of work in those press interviews.'

'Can we, please, get on with some work?' pleaded Mary with a sigh of exasperation. 'Dr Brooks, these are Dr Maynard's notes.'

'Thanks.' Adele took the bundle of notes. 'I'd better go and get started.'

It felt strange, going into Jeanette's consulting room and preparing to take surgery on her own, but she'd barely sat down at the desk and started to read the first patient's notes when there came a tap on the door and it opened to reveal Casey on the threshold. Her heart turned over.

'Just thought I'd check that you're OK,' he said.

Briefly she allowed her eyes to meet his then at something she saw there she looked quickly away, mindful of

her resolve not to encourage him in any way. 'I'm fine,
thank you,' she replied crisply.

She was aware of an air of puzzlement about him as if
he couldn't quite fathom this new approach of hers.

'Quite happy to go solo?' he asked.

'Quite,' she replied, then in a moment of weakness
added, 'Thank you.'

'Well, you know where I am if you need me.' He turned
and left the room.

If you need me, he'd said. She stared at the door. If only
he knew. But she mustn't let her mind go off down that
avenue again. She had a surgery to take—her first solo
surgery—and suddenly she was overcome by an attack of
nerves as the full weight of responsibility hit her. In an
attempt to overcome her fears she pressed the buzzer for
her first patient.

The list was long and varied, mainly made up of
Jeanette's patients who had come expecting to see their
regular GP. One or two, she gathered from the receptionists, had made other appointments when they'd found
Jeanette wasn't there, others were desperate and didn't
mind who they saw as their symptoms required immediate
relief, and yet others, whose condition was neither serious
nor who wanted to make other appointments, came out of
sheer curiosity—perhaps in the vague hope that this new
young doctor might shed fresh light on a chronic ailment.

The conditions in that first surgery ranged from a young
woman suffering from frequent and painful bouts of cys-
titis to an elderly man with chronic bronchitis, from a child
with an ear infection to a teenage girl with period pains
and finally a distraught woman whose husband had just
left her and their young children to set up home with her
best friend.

After surgery and a quick coffee in the staffroom to

steady her nerves after the anguish of her last patient, Adele took several of Jeanette's home visits, the remainder being shared between Casey and Toby. One of these visits was up on the Bowscombe Estate, a prospect that filled Adele with apprehension. Her fears proved to be unfounded, however, for when she parked her car in front of the same seedy shopping mall which she had visited with Casey and faced the same group of youths lolling against the railings, it was to find that two of Flo Procter's boys were part of the group. She wasn't sure which two they were but they recognised her and when the inevitable jeers and catcalls began they intervened.

'Leave 'er alone,' called one of them, Robbie maybe or perhaps it was Elton. 'She's OK, she is. That's Dr Brooks—she's Casey's bird and she saw to our Stevie.'

'Yeah,' said the other. 'He were banged up but she saw he were bad and got 'im to 'ospital, didn't you, Doc?'

'That's right.' Adele managed a nervous smile, deciding not to correct the status he had bestowed on her. 'I did. So how is Stevie now?' she added bravely as her courage grew.

'He's all right,' said the first youth. 'He's 'ome now. He'll be in court soon,' he added proudly.

'Oh, really?' Adele swallowed but as she walked across to the block of flats she was visiting she suddenly had a rather satisfying feeling of having been accepted by this community, partly because of having been the one to spot Stevie's condition and partly—and she suspected the greater part—because she was Casey's trainee. But whatever it was, it added to her confidence, leaving her with a certainty that when she emerged from the flats after seeing her patient, her car would not only still be there but would also be in one piece.

'How did your day go?' asked Casey later, after she had

completed her second surgery and was wading through a mountain of paperwork.

'All right—I think.' She was exhausted but she didn't want to let him know that.

'Any problems?'

'No, I don't think so.' She shook her head. 'It was all pretty much routine. I'll leave a list of notes and referrals for Jeanette to see.' She paused. 'Have we heard any more about Lara?'

'She's holding her own apparently,' Casey replied. 'I spoke to Jeanette earlier. She said Lara is still only semi-conscious and they won't know if there's been any lasting brain damage until after they've done a scan, which should be some time tomorrow.'

'And the other girl?'

'She's OK. She was discharged from hospital last night. I just wish—' his jaw tightened '—they could catch the lowlifes who supply the stuff to these kids.' He paused. 'Oh, by the way, did you know the police have made an arrest in connection with the murder case?'

'Yes.' Adele nodded. 'They were saying something about it in Reception. Was it the mother's boyfriend?'

'No, that's what people assumed but the guy they've arrested was a boyfriend of the girl herself—someone in his twenties who had been seeing her for some months.'

'But she was barely fifteen,' protested Adele as an image of the girl came into her mind as she had seen her lying beneath that makeshift tent on the edge of a rain-swept quarry.

'I know.' Casey took a deep breath. 'But it bears out what I said about not jumping to the obvious conclusion.' He paused and after a moment said, 'Do you fancy going for a drink somewhere?'

Her immediate reaction was to say yes, that there was

nothing she'd like better, but something stopped her. 'No, thanks,' she heard herself say. 'I have things to do.'

That look of puzzlement was back on his face as if he simply couldn't understand the new coolness that was suddenly between them. Then he shrugged and left her to her paperwork.

This coolness, probably imperceptible to anyone else, seemed to grow between Adele and Casey as the week progressed and Adele continued to take Jeanette's surgeries. It saddened her that it had to be so, leaving an ache in her heart that surprisingly bore no resemblance to the ache that Nigel had left there.

And then, with no hint of warning, a chain of events began which was to change everything. It started at the end of the week during an afternoon surgery when Cheryl phoned through to ask Adele if she would see Elvira Jackson.

'Does she have an appointment?' asked Adele, her heart sinking at the thought of what she might be asked to deal with, given Elvira's unpredictable nature.

'No, she doesn't,' Cheryl replied. 'She just wandered in like she always does, demanding to see a doctor. I explained that Dr Maynard isn't here but she didn't seem bothered. Normally I would ask Casey to see her but he's out on a call. I can't ask Toby because it's been agreed that Toby doesn't see Elvira and that only leaves Dr Fletcher or yourself. Dr Fletcher has only just started his surgery…'

'And I've nearly finished,' said Adele. 'OK, I'll see her. Let me see a couple more on my list then send her in.'

'Thanks, Doctor.' The relief in Cheryl's voice was only too obvious.

The following two patients were routine appointments, one for a blood-pressure check and the other for a follow-up prescription, and as the second patient left the room Adele pressed the buzzer, mentally bracing herself.

As on the previous occasion that Elvira had come to the surgery, she came straight into the room without knocking. She still had the same rather wild-looking appearance, with her flowing dark hair, her layers of drab grey clothing and the strange expression in those pale eyes.

'Hello, Elvira,' said Adele.

Elvira sank down onto a chair without answering, dumping her various bags and carriers onto the floor beside her, and as the grey knitted coat fell open Adele noticed that beneath the scarves there was a glimmer of some orange material.

'How can I help you, Elvira?' she asked, folding her hands together on the desk and hoping desperately that Elvira wasn't going to demand more pregnancy tests.

'I want you to make sure the baby's all right,' said Elvira.

'The baby…?' Adele frowned.

'Yes. This baby.' Elvira patted her stomach. 'I need you to listen with one of those trumpet things.'

For a moment Adele was thrown. There was no baby, neither was there likely to be in view of what Casey had told her concerning Elvira's infertility, but he'd also said they'd had many problems in the past with Elvira and that it was probably best to humour her. While she was still struggling over the best approach to take, Elvira stood up, picked up her bags and walked towards the examination room, tugging open the door then disappearing inside. Adele hesitated for a moment then, rising to her feet, took an obstetric trumpet from Jeanette's cupboard and followed her. No doubt humouring her was by far the best way right now. Later maybe she could have a word with

Elvira's psychiatric social worker warning her that it seemed Elvira had another of her fixations.

Still fully clothed, Elvira had hauled herself onto the examination couch and was lying there, staring at the ceiling. As Adele approached the couch Elvira pulled aside her coat and scarves and fumbled with the silky material of her orange top. It suddenly struck Adele that the top was very similar to the one she had bought for the Fletchers' dinner party, the one she had been unable to find either at the time or since. In fact, it was identical, with its pleated neckline edged with tiny crystal beads. No doubt Elvira had bought herself one from the same high street shop.

Pulling up the top, Elvira exposed her smooth, white stomach. 'Listen in there,' she demanded.

Dutifully Adele put the trumpet to Elvira's abdomen and listened, at the same time wondering what Casey would have done. Probably he would have refused, being quite adamant that there was no baby. On the other hand, it had been he who had said it best to humour Elvira.

'What can you hear?' demanded Elvira.

'Actually,' said Adele, straightening up, 'I can't hear anything, Elvira.'

'What are you saying?' Elvira struggled into a sitting position.

'Only that I can't hear anything,' Adele replied truthfully.

'You're saying there isn't a baby,' said Elvira. Pulling her clothes around her, she slid from the couch, gathered up her various bags and plastic carriers and stalked out of the examination room and then out of the consulting room.

Adele followed her to the door. 'Elvira…' she called after the woman's retreating figure, but Elvira failed even to turn and with a sigh Adele went back into the room and sat down once more at the desk.

She was far from satisfied with how she had dealt with the situation but she wasn't quite sure what else she could have done, given the circumstances. Lifting the telephone receiver, she asked Cheryl if Elvira had left the surgery.

'Yes,' Cheryl answered, 'she's just swept out. Did you have a problem with her?'

'Not exactly, but I think I'd like a word with her psychiatric social worker. Could you get her for me, please?'

'Yes, of course,' Cheryl replied. 'That'll be Ruby Felton.'

Adele held the line and Ruby came on within a couple of minutes. 'Dr Brooks?' she said. 'How may I help you?'

'It's probably nothing, Ruby,' said Adele. 'But I've just had Elvira Jackson in.'

'Do we have a problem looming?' asked Ruby.

'I think we might,' Adele replied. 'Unfortunately Elvira thinks she's pregnant.'

'Oh, dear, no, not again,' sighed Ruby.

'I had heard this has happened before.'

'Yes, about a year ago. Elvira will have quite long stretches of time where she's absolutely fine—that's when she remembers to take her medication. If she forgets or refuses to take it we usually have a problem, more often than not some sort of fixation. If it gets out of hand Elvira could then become a danger to herself and to others.'

'Where is she living these days?' asked Adele.

'She's in a hostel. I think I'll call in later today and check up on her medication.'

'Thanks, Ruby, I'd appreciate that.' Adele was relieved.

'Not at all. It should be me thanking you. You've probably tipped me off in good time before things get out of hand.'

Adele put the phone down, feeling decidedly better than she had when Elvira had stalked out of the room, and by the time she'd finished her surgery she'd almost managed to put Elvira out of her mind.

On returning to Reception with the patients' records, she found a debate going on between Penny, Cheryl and Lizzie over what Penny was going to wear that evening.

'I think the black for where you're going,' said Cheryl, standing back and eyeing Penny up and down as if she were wearing the garment she had in mind instead of her nursing uniform.

'But I think it makes me look fat!' wailed Penny.

'No, it doesn't,' said Cheryl. 'Black is slimming, isn't it?' she added, looking at Adele for support.

'Er, yes, I suppose it is,' Adele agreed.

'Not that she'd know,' said Lizzie with a sniff. 'I'll bet she's never had to lose weight in her life.'

'No, not really,' Adele admitted. 'In fact, at one time when I was in my teens I was actually trying to put a little weight on.'

'Doesn't it just make you sick?' sighed Penny. 'I know after tonight I shall probably have to go back to my slimming club. Honestly, I only have to look at a slice of cheesecake and it settles on my hips. Which makes me wonder whether I should wear the cream trousers. They do make my hips look thinner…whereas the black…'

Suddenly Adele couldn't bear to listen to any more. It was pretty obvious that Penny had a date that evening and it stood to reason that date was with Casey. She didn't want to hear about it, about what Penny intended wearing or where they were going, because if she did, she knew that for the rest of the night she would carry in her head

images of a romantic, intimate meal for two in some se-
cluded restaurant together with what would inevitably follow.

Out of the corner of her eye she saw Casey coming
through the front entrance and with a muttered excuse she
hurried out of Reception, passing Casey with barely more
than a nod as she made her way outside and round the
building to the entrance to the flats.

Wearily she trailed up the stairs, angry with herself for
feeling the way she did. She should be happy for Penny
and Casey—and she was, wasn't she? she asked herself
firmly as she inserted her key in the lock and opened the
door of her flat.

The first thing that struck her was that something was
different. It was darker than usual—the muslin curtains
drawn together, shutting out the light. Surely she hadn't
left them like that when she'd left the flat that morning?
The second thing, to her amazement, was that there were
candles burning—on the coffee-table, the mantelpiece and
the bureau. Although she often lit candles, she knew for
certain she hadn't left any burning that day and even if
she had, they would have burnt out in the time she had
been away.

With a muttered exclamation she started forward and as
she did so the door shut behind her with a loud click,
which caused her to turn sharply. A figure was sitting in
the chair behind the door. In shock Adele saw that it was
Elvira.

CHAPTER ELEVEN

'ELVIRA!' Adele's mouth suddenly went dry. 'What are you doing here?'

Elvira stared steadily back at her. 'I live here,' she said. 'This is my flat.'

'No, Elvira.' Adele struggled to stay calm. 'This is my flat. It used to be yours,' she added hastily when she saw Elvira's nostrils flare, 'but it's mine now. You live at the hostel.'

'I live here,' said Elvira, deliberately emphasising each word.

'How did you get in?' Adele frowned, knowing for a fact that she'd locked the door that morning as she did every morning when she left the flat.

'With my key, of course.' Elvira's lip curled in derision. 'How d'you think I got in?'

'I didn't know you had a key.'

'Of course I have. I had a spare one cut.'

Adele stared at her. 'But didn't you hand it over with the other keys when you left?' she asked at last.

'Why should I?' Elvira demanded. 'It's mine. I paid for it. I needed it to get into my flat.'

For a moment Adele was speechless. An awful possibility began to form in her mind and she said, 'Have you been in here before, Elvira? Since you've been staying at the hostel?'

'Oh, yes.' Elvira's strange, pale eyes shone in the candlelight. 'I can't get in at night because they lock the outside door, but during the day when you're all busy down-stairs I come up here.'

Suddenly the hairs at the back of Adele's neck stood on end as it became clear what Elvira was saying, and at the same moment she knew with indisputable certainty that the orange top Elvira was wearing was the one she herself had bought and been unable to find. From what Elvira had just said, it sounded as if she'd let herself into the flat, rummaged through her possessions and taken the top. And it seemed as if that hadn't been the only occasion. If what she'd said was true, it would appear she had been here in the flat many times while Adele had been working.

Fighting a sudden wave of rising panic, Adele somehow hung onto her sanity, knowing the only way out of this was to humour the woman. 'I think,' she said, her gaze flickering briefly to the door, 'I'll just pop down to the surgery again. I left some notes down there—'

'No, you won't.' Elvira's voice was like a whiplash. 'You'll tell them I'm here and they'll make me go back to the hostel. I'm not going back,' she said determinedly, 'and you're not going anywhere either. I need you here to deliver my baby.'

'Your baby…?' Adele swallowed, wondering how on earth she could get out of this desperate situation.

'It'll be born soon.' Elvira nodded. 'See, I've started to get ready. I've lit all the candles…you'll have to boil the water. They always have boiling water.'

Adele stared at her. 'Yes, of course…the water,' she said at last. Turning, she moved into the kitchen.

With shaking hands she filled the kettle, plugged it in and flicked the switch. There was no sound from the main room and as she waited for the water to boil she leaned across the sink unit and peered out of the window. The kitchen overlooked the courtyard—maybe, if she was careful, she could attract someone's attention. Even as the possibility entered her head Toby's car drew into the courtyard. Adele sucked in her breath then as quietly as she could she gently lifted the window catch and pushed open the window.

As Toby stepped out of his car she braced herself to shout.

'Get away from that window!' She turned sharply to find Elvira behind her, and in that instant while she was thrown off her guard Elvira leaned forward and pulled the window shut. It made a noise and from where Adele was standing she could see that Toby glanced up before disappearing from their view into the house. Even now he would be making his way up the stairs to his own flat on the first floor, totally unaware of the drama being played out above him.

With a little gasp of despair Adele turned to find Elvira so close that her face was only inches from her own. She was vaguely aware that she had something in her hand but she was so close that for a moment she was unable to see what it was.

'Don't even think about any funny business!' hissed Elvira. 'You have a job to do.'

There was a click and a flame flared in Adele's face. As she felt the heat she recoiled in horror as she realised that the object in Elvira's hand was a cigarette lighter.

'If you make any trouble I'll set fire to your hair.' Elvira spoke quietly but with so much menace that Adele in a moment of sheer terror didn't for one moment doubt that she would carry out her threat if the desire took her to do so.

Humour her, she heard Casey say in her mind. Humour her. That might have been relatively easy in a crowded surgery—it was something else entirely up here, alone, at the top of the house with a disturbed woman who had a tendency towards pyromania.

'We're not leaving here till you deliver my baby.' Elvira extinguished the flame but the light in her eyes burned as fiercely as ever. 'So you might as well get that into your head now.'

In a desperate effort to pull herself together Adele took a deep breath. She knew that everything depended on how she handled the situation with this very disturbed woman. Slowly she followed Elvira back into the living room where the other woman resumed her position on the seat behind the door. Gingerly Adele perched herself on the edge of the sofa and for a period of time, the length of which she found impossible to determine—and as all around them the candles flickered and burned lower—they remained that way, waiting presumably for Elvira to announce the imminent arrival of her baby.

And then, slowly at first but gathering momentum and in a more determined fashion, Elvira began rocking herself back and forth in her chair and muttering under her breath. Once or twice Adele caught the word 'Nash' and remembered that Casey had told her that Elvira had had a fixation with Toby in the past. She wondered if in her own mind Elvira thought that Toby was the father of the baby she believed she was carrying.

Adele knew that if she didn't do something the situation could well go on all night, but the only other way to attract attention would be by phone. She had already ruled out using the main phone, which was in full view of Elvira, but in her pocket she carried her mobile phone. Maybe, if she could get away from Elvira's gaze for just a few moments, she could text a message to Casey whose own mobile number was programmed into her phone. But getting away from Elvira was going to be the biggest problem.

Humour her, Casey had said. Previously, Adele had doubted the wisdom of going along with the pretence of the baby. Now, as she gradually reached the conclusion that it could offer the solution she needed, she had no such qualms.

'Do you have a name for the baby?' she asked after a while. She struggled to keep her tone casual, matter-of-fact, just as if she were talking to a patient in the antenatal clinic.

Elvira, however, chose not to answer, instead increasing the momentum of her rocking action. Adele decided to continue with the strategy she had chosen.

'I was just wondering,' she said, looking around the room, 'where we'll put baby after it's born. I could clear out a drawer, or on second thoughts the bed might be better—the sheets were clean on this morning and we do have to make sure everything is clean. Speaking of which, I'll need to scrub up if I'm to deliver a baby.' She stood up and, keeping a wary eye on Elvira, moved towards the bathroom. Elvira seemed oblivious to her and carried on with her rocking movement, all the while muttering to herself.

Once inside the bathroom Adele didn't dare to shut the door, let alone lock it, afraid if she did so that Elvira's mood might change again and she might see fit to set fire to goodness knows what, endangering the safety of them both in this top-floor flat. Instead, she turned on both taps and, picking up a nailbrush in her left hand, began a scrubbing movement against her leg. With her right hand she carefully withdrew her mobile phone from her pocket and under cover of the sound of scrubbing and of running water she compiled a text message to Casey. All she put was, 'Elvira. My flat. Dangerous.' Then she sent the message, slipped the phone back into her pocket and washed her hands before turning the taps off.

When she returned to the living area she was wiping her hands on a towel. Elvira was in exactly the same position but her gaze very briefly flickered in Adele's direction. Adele noticed that one of the candles had gone out and another two were flickering wildly. She wondered whether she should offer to light more. The last thing she wanted was for Elvira to start waving her lighter around again, but in the end she thought better of it. While being attracted to fire herself, Elvira might well resent anyone else's control over it.

'Well,' Adele said brightly, resuming her seat on the sofa, 'that's that. We're all ready now for baby's arrival.'

Elvira stopped rocking and looked levelly at Adele, and Adele found herself holding her breath. 'What baby?' she almost snarled the words.

'Your baby, of course, Elvira,' said Adele, endeavouring to keep a smile on her face but she feared, failing miserably as she felt it degenerate into a grimace. 'The baby you're expecting.'

'You silly cat!' spat Elvira. 'I'm not having a baby.'

'You're not?' said Adele weakly.

'Course I'm not. How dare you say I'm having a baby? That's filthy, that is. I never let no one touch me.' Elvira's voice began to rise hysterically.

'All right, Elvira,' said Adele more calmly than she was feeling. 'You're not going to have a baby.'

Desperately she wished Casey would come. Had he got her message? Had he gone out with Penny already or had she caught him before they went? The clock read ten past seven which meant she had been here with Elvira for just over an hour. It seemed longer than that—much longer. Supposing Casey hadn't got the message, what then?

Would they be here all night? She shuddered at the thought and as Elvira began to get increasingly restless and Adele was on the edge of despair, wondering what on earth she could do next, the door was suddenly flung back on its hinges and the room was full of people.

Casey was there in his battered leather jacket, there were policemen in uniform and Ruby Felton, Elvira's social worker, was with them. What happened next was to become a blur in Adele's mind. She was vaguely aware that Elvira was being examined by Casey who gave her an injection then, accompanied by Ruby, she was led away by the police until in the end there was only herself and Casey left in the flat together with one policeman.

'Are you all right, Dr Brooks?' The policeman crouched down in front of Adele who was still sitting on the sofa.

'Yes, I'm fine, thanks,' Adele lied automatically. She wasn't really fine. She had started to shake, her throat was dry and her stomach was churning.

'Can you tell me exactly what happened here?' The policeman was very young and not one whom she'd seen at the police station.

'She was here when I came up to the flat.' Adele clenched her hands, digging her nails into her palms in an attempt to stop them shaking.

'So had she broken in?' The policeman was writing now in a spiral-bound notebook.

'She said she had a key.' Adele swallowed. 'She said she had one cut.' Casey drew in his breath sharply and Adele threw him a quick glance. His expression was grim, his jaw taut and his mouth set in an uncompromising line.

'Will you be wanting to bring any charges?' asked the policeman.

Adele shook her head. 'I shouldn't think so,' she said. 'She's a patient and she was very disturbed.'

'Can we discuss this later?' said Casey.

'Yes, of course.' The policeman straightened up and closed his notebook. 'We'll be wanting a statement from you, Dr Brooks, next time you're down at the station.'

He departed, leaving Adele and Casey alone.

'Are you really all right?' Casey turned to Adele as the door shut behind the policeman.

'Yes, I think so…' She attempted to stand up and as her legs threatened to give out, she would have stumbled if Casey hadn't steadied her.

'Hey,' he said softly, 'you're not all right, are you?' He continued to hold her.

'I seem to be making a habit of this sort of thing,' she said shakily. 'Last time it was certifying a death, this time it's…well, I don't really know what you'd call this. All I know is that she frightened me to death.'

'You say she had a key?' Casey lowered his head slightly to look into her face.

'Yes.' Adele nodded. 'She said she'd had one cut when she was living here.'

Casey looked quite stricken. 'We should have changed the locks. So what happened?' Slowly he sat down on the sofa and drew Adele down beside him, all the while keeping one arm around her.

'She came to surgery,' Adele explained slowly. 'I was the only one available so I told Cheryl I would see her. She was still fixed on the fact that she was having a baby—she wanted me to listen for the heartbeat.'

'So did you?' Casey's eyes narrowed.

'Yes, but I told her I couldn't hear anything,' Adele replied. When Casey nodded, as if in approval, she went on, 'But that seemed to annoy her. She walked out of the surgery. I was concerned about her state of mind so I rang Ruby Felton. Ruby said to leave it with her and that she would call at the hostel where Elvira is living and check that she's taking her medication. I was happy with that but later after surgery when I came up to the flat I found that—' her voice wavered as she relived that awful moment '—Elvira had let herself in.'

'What state of mind was she in at that point?' asked Casey.

Briefly Adele told him about how Elvira had thought that this was still her flat, of how she wanted her, Adele, to stay there and deliver her baby and of how she had lit all the candles in the flat.

He interrupted her only once. 'Did she threaten you?'

Adele took a deep breath then nodded. 'Yes, when I tried to attract Toby's attention out of the window. She'd followed me into the kitchen and she threatened to set fire…to my hair.' She turned and looked at him as she spoke and saw the brief look of horror that passed across his features.

'Did she have matches?' His arm tightened around her.

'No, a cigarette lighter.' Adele shuddered at the memory. 'I don't doubt she would have done it but I managed to get her back in here and we sat for ages, but when I started talking about the baby again…you know, to try and humour her, she didn't seem to know what I was talking about. It was pretty scary, I can tell you…'

'I'm sure it was.' Casey ran a hand over his hair in a distracted fashion. 'Hell, it must have been a nightmare.'

'It was…rather,' Adele gulped. 'And another thing, and I have to say this really freaked me out—she was wearing one of my tops.'

'What?' Casey frowned. 'You mean she went through your things before you came up here?'

'No.' Adele shook her head. 'It was worse than that. She'd been in here before and taken it. She was wearing it when she came to the surgery. At that point, even though mine had gone missing I thought it was just a similar one, but after finding her here and realising that she'd had a key all this time I knew it was mine and that she'd been here before. I...I don't know how many times...but I tell you, it's really scary, thinking back over and just wondering when she might have been in here.' She paused, reflecting.

'She said she would come here while we were working during the day,' she continued after a while. 'Presumably she couldn't get in at night because the outer door would have been locked and bolted.' She clenched her hands again. 'That's something, I suppose—the thought of her getting in here at night simply doesn't bear thinking about.' Falling silent again, she dwelt on the awful possibility of that then after a while she went on, 'It's made me wonder about other things. Like when I first moved in, I found food in the fridge. I thought at the time that it might have been Penny or Rosie but when I asked them neither of them knew anything about it. I guess that must have been Elvira as well. Goodness knows what other things she did. She probably went through all my things— my letters, my clothes, everything...'

Casey, while continuing to hold her closely against him, had grown very quiet and when she turned towards him questioningly, he said, 'Actually, I have a bit of a confession to make...'

'A confession?' She frowned.

'Yes.' He hesitated, as if uncertain how to continue, then he said, 'It wasn't Elvira who put the food in the fridge— it was me.'

'You!' She stared at him in amazement.

'Yes.' He nodded in an embarrassed sort of way. 'I thought, well, I thought it would be by way of a welcome,

I suppose. I guess I was feeling a bit guilty. I'd opposed the idea of a trainee and in the end I'd been forced into being the one to take on your training. I wasn't too happy about that and I knew I would have to make a real effort if I wasn't to let my attitude show...'

'And there was me being really off with you when I first arrived,' said Adele slowly, 'saying you didn't look like a doctor and telling you that you couldn't park in the court-yard...'

'Yes, you were a bit uppity,' agreed Casey with a sudden grin. As always the smile transformed his features, giving a brief glimpse of the man beneath the tough exterior he presented to the world.

While they'd been talking they'd gradually relaxed, moving farther back into the comfort of the sofa's many cushions, and all the while Casey's arm had remained protectively around her. It had felt good, warm and safe, and she'd had not the slightest desire to push him away, but now, as the terrors of her ordeal faded a little and the reality sank in that the danger was over, the incongruity of their situation finally hit her.

Very gradually Adele began to ease herself away from him, but even though she succeeded in putting a little distance between them his arm remained along the back of the sofa.

'I'm all right now, Casey,' she said at last, a little uneasily. 'I mustn't keep you any longer.' Really, there wasn't anything she would have liked better—for him to stay there with her for the rest of the evening, or even the night. But, no, she mustn't even entertain such thoughts, intriguing as they might be.

'I'm not in any hurry.' Casey leaned back on the sofa, stretching out his legs before him and linking his hands behind his head.

'But aren't you going to be late?' Adele half turned and looked at him, surprised at his apparent lack of urgency. She wasn't sure what time his date with Penny was but it had to be soon.

'Late for what?' He'd closed his eyes and he answered without opening them.

'Well, your date,' she said uncertainly, wondering whether in the heat of the moment he might have simply forgotten. Surely now he would leap up and beat a hasty retreat to his own flat to change into appropriate wear to take Penny to the restaurant she had been talking about earlier?

'I wasn't aware I had a date.' He opened one eye and looked at her.

'But I thought…I thought you and Penny had a date this evening…'

'I can't imagine why you would have thought that.'

'Well, I thought… Penny was talking to the girls earlier about what she was going to wear for her date this evening.'

'So why should you have thought her date was with me?' He'd opened both eyes now and, lowering his arms and easing himself into an upright position, he stared at her.

'Well, you and Penny are an item…aren't you?' Adele felt she was rapidly in danger of losing the plot.

'Do you know,' he said, 'you're the second person recently who was under that same impression.'

'Am I?' she asked faintly.

'Yes.' He nodded. 'Toby thought the same thing.'

'Toby…?' Suddenly this whole conversation seemed in danger of spiralling right out of control.

'Yes. Toby seemed to think that Penny and I had a thing going. I can't imagine how these rumours start.' He shook his head as if the whole thing was beyond him. 'And then,' he went on, 'when I put Toby right he seemed not only amazed but utterly delighted. It appears he had wanted to ask Penny out but hadn't because he thought she was seeing me. In fact, I think you'll find it's Toby who has the date with Penny tonight.'

'I don't understand.' Adele stared at him but somewhere deep inside a little throb of excitement had begun. 'I thought you and Penny were an item. I've thought it ever since I arrived. It was me who told Toby that you were—'

'Ah, so it was you who started the rumour.' There was a look of exasperated amusement on his face now. 'But I have to say I can't think why. Whatever gave you that impression?'

'It was Penny herself who told me.' Adele was thoroughly bewildered now. 'The day I arrived she came in here to welcome me and she confided in me that you and she were a bit of an item. She said it was only early days but that she was hopeful that it was going somewhere.' She paused and saw that Casey had grown very still. 'So what was all that about?' she asked. 'Why would Penny have thought that?'

'I can only think,' he said at last, 'that it was something to do with the fact that I took her out to dinner.'

'You took Penny out to dinner?'

'Yes,' he said. 'It was by way of showing appreciation. She'd given me a hand when I moved in here—cooked me a couple of meals, that sort of thing—and I just thought it was a gesture, that's all. I had no idea she'd misconstrued it. When Toby mentioned it, I just thought he'd been mistaken and when he said that he'd fancied Penny for a long time I told him to go ahead and ask her out. But now that you've said this I wonder if perhaps I'd better speak to Penny and clear up any misunderstanding.'

'So there was never anything between you?' asked Adele softly.

'Of course not.' He stared at her then in further exasperation he said, 'Don't get me wrong. Penny's a lovely girl but she isn't my type—it's as simple as that.'

Suddenly Adele longed to ask him just exactly what was his type but she didn't quite dare and in the end she didn't have to, for right out of the blue Casey suddenly leaned forward and said, 'You're my type, Adele.'

'Am I?' she said, delighted but startled by his bluntness.

'I thought I'd made that only too obvious,' he said ruefully. 'In the end I backed off because I thought you weren't ready for another relationship yet.'

'And I kept you at arm's length because I thought you were two-timing Penny,' said Adele incredulously.

'You mean…you, too?' he said, his eyes widening.

'Oh, yes,' she replied softly.

A variety of emotions passed across his features and after a moment he said, 'I couldn't believe it when you turned up with Toby at Celia's party, especially after you'd made it plain to me that you weren't into relationships at the moment.'

'You acted as if you were jealous.' Adele raised one eyebrow.

'Maybe I was at that,' he said quietly, and suddenly the idea of him being jealous of Toby stirred some basic emotion deep inside her.

They were silent for a while, each reflecting on what had happened, then Casey rose to his feet and, taking her hands, drew her up beside him. 'I have a suggestion to make,' he said.

Adele looked up at him and her heart lurched at the expression she saw in his eyes.

'What's that?' she whispered.

'I suggest we start again—as if we'd just met. I'll speak to Penny and make sure there are no misunderstandings. I want you to be sure you're over Nigel and happy about starting another relationship, and I'll have a word with Edward and make sure there are no ethical complications with a trainer and his trainee becoming an item. How does that sound to you?'

'It sounds wonderful,' she said simply. 'Just let me know when you've sorted it all out.'

Slowly he leaned forward and very gently touched her lips with his. It had none of the fire or passion of that last time but it carried tenderness beyond her wildest dreams and more than the hint of a promise of what might be to come.

CHAPTER TWELVE

AT FIRST Adele could hardly believe it was happening. 'We'll take it slowly,' Casey had said, and they did, allowing their initial attraction for each other to grow into a delicious awareness of one another. For Adele, the fact that Casey and Penny weren't an item, and furthermore never had been, had come as a wonderful revelation. She was anxious at first as to how Penny would react when Casey spoke to her but she needn't have worried.

'She was fine,' he told her in response to her worried questions. 'She'd thought that maybe we could get together after the meal we'd had but she'd realised in the last few weeks that it wasn't going to happen.'

'What about her and Toby?'

'Well, that does look as if it might be going somewhere. Toby's leaping about like a two-year-old and Penny looks, well, I don't know what the word is…'

'Radiant?' suggested Adele.

Casey frowned. 'Yes, I suppose you could call it that,' he agreed at last. 'Radiant.'

Adele smiled. 'And what about us?' she asked softly. They were in Casey's consulting room at the time. She was perched on the edge of the desk and he was seated alongside her in his chair.

'What about us?' he asked, reaching out and covering her knee with his hand. His touch sent shock waves through her body and she was forced to struggle to concentrate on what she was saying when really she would have liked nothing better than to slide along the desk and into his lap.

'Did you tell her about us?' she asked, ignoring the clamouring of her body.

'Yes, I did,' Casey confessed.

'How did she take it?'

'In my experience, those who are in love have nothing but generosity towards others.'

'You mean she didn't mind?'

'On the contrary. She said she wasn't surprised, that she'd suspected it might happen from the moment you arrived.'

'Maybe that was why she warned me off on that very first day,' said Adele slowly.

'Yes, maybe,' Casey agreed, 'but whatever, we needn't worry about that any more.'

'And what about Edward?' Adele leaned forward slightly. 'Have you told him yet?'

'Ah, yes, Edward. Now, that was a bit more of a worry.' Removing his hand from her knee, Casey rubbed his fingers over his forehead, the gesture somehow both boyish and endearing.

'Was there a problem?' asked Adele quickly. 'Did he object?'

'Not object exactly.' Casey shook his head. 'In fact, when I first told him I would have said his initial reaction was one of delight, but since then he's seemed a little more…well, guarded I suppose you'd call it.'

'Has he said why?'

'Not really.' Casey shrugged. 'He did imply that it mustn't affect our work in any way and I suppose he does have a point there. Neither would he want too much gossip…'

'Probably there will only be gossip and speculation

whilst people don't know for sure,' said Adele slowly. 'Maybe once they do know it won't matter to them.'

'Maybe,' Casey agreed, then he added, 'But perhaps at least for the time being it might be an idea to keep it low-key whilst the others are around.' He must have seen her look of disappointment. 'Don't get me wrong,' he added hurriedly, 'I would like to shout it from the housetops, but I don't want anything to compromise your position here.'

'OK.' Adele nodded.

'We'll make up for it behind closed doors,' he added softly.

'Oh, yes,' she murmured. He looked faintly anxious and, reaching out her hand, she gently smoothed his forehead as if to eradicate the lines of tension. At the same time she smoothed his eyebrow which, as ever, was ruffled by the deep line of his scar. 'Tell me,' she said in the same soft tone. 'I've been dying to ask ever since we met. How did you get this?'

'How do you think I might have got it?' There was a hint of amusement in his voice now as his brow cleared.

'I thought probably in those wild days of your youth, in a fight between rival gangs, maybe over a girl...'

He laughed, throwing his head back. 'Nothing so romantic, I can assure you,' he said.

'Then how?'

'I came off a motorbike. Years ago. Wet night, sharp bend.' He shrugged. 'These things happen. There, now, you're disappointed, aren't you?'

'Not exactly. I just thought...' It was her turn to laugh and that was how Cheryl found them as she tapped on the door and opened it without waiting for an answer—Adele sitting on the desk facing Casey, both laughing.

'Oh, I'm sorry.' Cheryl looked from one to the other

with barely concealed interest. 'I just wanted some sig-
natures.'

'So much for keeping it quiet,' said Casey ruefully after
Cheryl had gone. 'She couldn't wait to get back to the
others to tell them.'

'Well.' Adele slipped down from the desk. 'From now
on we'll be models of discretion.'

And they were. During surgery hours anyway, whether
in their consulting rooms, in the staffroom, on house calls
or if they both attended a police call-out. But when they
were off duty it was a different matter as they spent more
and more time together. Within a very short space of time
Adele knew she was falling deeply in love with Casey.

'Am I always to call you that?' she asked one day as
they walked together in the woods behind Stourborne
Abbas.

'I would prefer that you do,' he replied.

'So do I get to know the first name you so despise?'
She looked up at him from beneath her lashes.

'It isn't so much that I despise it,' he said stiffly. 'It was
simply that I got fed up with people's reactions when they
hear it for the first time.'

'And what reaction is that?'

'Oh, they laugh,' he said wryly. 'Every time they laugh.'

'So try me,' she said. 'I promise I won't laugh. Neither
will I tell.'

He was silent for a moment, as if hesitating over
whether to tell her or not. It was a misty, autumn morning
and to the accompaniment of distant church bells they had
tramped for miles across fields damp with dew before entering the splendid silence of the woods where all around
the trees were turning to glorious shades of gold, russet
and copper.

'Let me try and guess,' she said playfully at last, tugging at his hand.

'Go on, then.' His eyes were serious but a smile played around the corners of his mouth.

'Well, I know it begins with H,' she began slowly.

'How do you know that?' He sounded indignant and she laughed.

'I just do, that's all. Let me see—is it Horace?'

'Of course not.'

'Oh, well.' She shrugged. That put paid to Elaine's theory. 'How about Hannibal?'

'No!' He gave a barely disguised shudder.

'Hamish, then, or Horatio or Hornblower.'

He didn't answer and she flashed him a quick look. 'Am I right?' she demanded. 'Is it one of those? Hornblower?'

'Not Hornblower.' He shook his head. 'And I have to say I wouldn't have minded if it was Hamish.'

'Horatio?' She raised her eyebrows and he nodded miserably.

'Oh, but, Casey…' She stopped, forcing him to do the same. When he turned to face her she took his other hand and looked up at him. 'There's nothing wrong with Horatio. It's a fine, noble name—the name of a hero!'

'You try explaining that to a classroom full of boys when you have to call out your name,' he said gloomily.

'How did it come about?' she asked.

'My mother had a thing about Nelson and Lady Hamilton.'

'I think that's incredibly romantic.'

'OK.' He shrugged, then with a scowl added, 'Just as long as you carry on calling me Casey.'

'Of course I will.' Reaching up, Adele wound her arms around his neck. His kiss as his lips met hers was gentle, full of tenderness, then as passion flared between them, consuming them in a fierce sense of urgency, it grew deeper and more demanding.

That night for the first time they made love. After returning from their walk, Casey cooked supper for them both in his apartment then they lay together on the sofa, listening to music. They had both known all day what was going to happen and when at last, much later, he stood up and, taking her hand, led her to his bedroom it was with a satisfying sense of inevitability. He undressed her slowly in that calm, unhurried way that she had come to associate with him, savouring each moment as if each action and its revelation were precious beyond price. When she was naked he discarded his own clothes, but rapidly this time, letting them fall to the floor before joining her on the bed.

His love-making was passionate and exciting, just as Adele had imagined it might be, arousing her to fever pitch then showing a tender restraint that rendered her almost helpless with impatience.

'We have all night,' he murmured once, and she was forced to wait.

Finally he took her to a place she had never been, from a plateau of longing and desire to a pinnacle of unutterable fulfilment before a long, slow, shuddering descent to reality.

She knew she called his name then clung to him in the darkness, almost sobbing with relief before finally drifting into a deep, dreamless sleep.

In the morning when Adele awoke to bright sunlight she couldn't for a moment think where she was. As memory came flooding back she turned her head, but Casey was no longer beside her. Suddenly she felt bereft, but even as she wondered he came into the bedroom wearing a white towelling robe and bearing two mugs of tea on a tray.

'Good morning.' His gaze met hers.

'Hello,' she said almost shyly, as she suddenly recalled her uninhibited demands of the night before. She sat up, pushing her hair back from her face.

'I trust you slept well.' He sat beside her, passing her one of the mugs.

'Oh, yes.' She smiled, sipping her tea. It was hot and sweet, exactly the way she liked it.

'I just have time for this,' he said, sipping his own tea, 'then I have a call-out.'

'Do you?' She was disappointed. She'd been hoping he would get back into bed so that they could maybe enjoy another half-hour or so together before going down to the surgery.

'Yes, Maudie isn't too well. I just had a call from Flo. I told her I'd go before surgery.'

'OK.' She set her mug down on the bedside table and stretched. 'Do you want me to come with you?'

'No.' He grinned then gently touched her cheek. 'You get yourself sorted out.'

He was gone almost before she knew it. One moment he was there beside her and it seemed the next he was dressed and gone and she was alone in his apartment. But wasn't that what being a doctor entailed? Wouldn't it always be like that, with one or the other of them constantly at the beck and call of the public? With a little sigh Adele finished her tea then slipped out of bed and headed for the shower.

She had a busy day ahead of her. Jeanette was due back at work following the news that Lara hadn't suffered any brain damage, so she would need to go through all the notes of the patients she had seen in Jeanette's absence. And as if that wasn't enough, Edward had said he wanted a couple of days off so she would be covering his surgeries as well.

The day proved to be every bit as hectic as she had feared and it seemed to set the pattern for the remainder of that week. She and Casey snatched moments together whenever they could, but their special time continued to be the nights, which they spent in one or the other of their flats.

One evening when briefly she was alone Adele had a call from her sister.

'Lainey!' she exclaimed when she heard her sister's voice. 'I've been meaning to call you, but somehow I just don't seem to have got round to it. How are you?'

'I'm fine,' her sister replied brightly. Too brightly, thought Adele, who knew her very well. 'More to the point, how are you?'

'Yes, er, pretty good. What's wrong, Lainey?'

'What do you mean, what's wrong?' Elaine sounded indignant now, on the defensive.

'Well, I always know when there's something wrong, so you might as well get it over and tell me what it is.'

She heard her sister's sigh. 'Well, actually...yes, you're right, there is something. I might as well tell you because you'll find out sooner or later anyway. There's not really any easy way of saying this...'

'Oh, do get on with it, Lainey,' said Adele impatiently. 'You're getting me really worried now. It isn't Mum, is it?'

'No, no, it isn't Mum. Nothing like that,' said Elaine hastily. 'It's just that there's an announcement in this morning's *Times* about Nigel's marriage. Apparently he and Lucinda were married a week ago.'

'Nigel?' Adele said coolly, and she surprised even herself at just how coolly. 'Nigel who?'

There was silence from the other end of the line and

Adele found herself smiling as she imagined her sister's expression.

'Well, Nigel.' Elaine sounded bewildered now. 'Your Nigel, of course.'

'He isn't my Nigel.'

'Well, no, I know he isn't now but, well, he was, wasn't he?' The indignant note was back in Elaine's voice.

'Yes, Lainey, he was,' agreed Adele. 'But that's history now. I wish him well—he and Lucinda were made for each other.'

'Well.' Elaine sounded astonished. 'That's very generous of you, I'm sure. I don't think I could have been so charitable under the circumstances…unless… Del, do I detect the presence of another man in your life?' she demanded suddenly.

'How did you guess?' Adele chuckled.

Elaine gave a shriek and Adele nearly dropped the phone. 'Oh, wonderful!' she cried. 'Who is it? No, don't tell me, let me guess. Is it that hunky trainer of yours—the one with the leathers and the motorbike?'

'Right first time,' said Adele dryly, but her heart had leapt at even her sister's description of Casey.

'Oh, Del, I'm so happy for you!' Elaine was almost babbling now. 'So, do you think this is it?' she asked eagerly.

'Oh, I hope so, Lainey,' Adele replied. 'I do hope so because I've never been so happy in all my life.'

It was perfectly true what Adele had told her sister. She had never been so happy before. Casey had added a new dimension to her life, showing her a love of depth and tenderness that she hadn't even touched on with Nigel. In spite of their agreement to keep their relationship as low-key as possible in front of the other members of staff,

Adele's radiance must have been only too obvious to those around her. To her delight Penny's and Toby's romance also seemed to be flourishing.

'This love lark must be catching,' muttered Cheryl one morning in Reception.

'Oh, I hope so,' said Lizzie, leaning over the desk and watching as Penny and Toby lingered together in the foyer before he went off to do his house calls. 'Because whatever it is those two are on—I'd like some.'

Adele and Casey were behind the desk, signing prescriptions, and they both looked up at the comments. As their gazes met, Adele felt the colour flood her cheeks and Casey's lips twitched.

'What do *you* think, Adele?' Cheryl obviously hadn't finished.

'Me?' Adele's voice came out in a startled squawk. 'Oh, I wouldn't know,' she said hastily.

'Yeah, right.' Cheryl turned to answer the phone and Adele was saved from further embarrassment by the arrival of Ruby.

'Ruby, hello!' It was Casey who hailed the social worker, almost as if he was also glad of a diversion in the direction the conversation was taking. 'What news of Elvira?'

'Elvira is doing well. She's still in hospital but she's responding well to a new drug regime. Oh, and you'll be pleased to know I've sorted out new housing arrangements for her in sheltered accommodation. There will be someone on hand to make sure she takes her medication but she'll still retain a good level of independence.'

'Well, that's a relief,' said Lizzie, 'and I'm sure Adele will agree with that.'

'Absolutely.' Adele nodded.

'Keep us posted on Elvira, Ruby,' said Casey. 'When

she comes out of hospital one of us will visit, either myself or Jeanette.'

A few moments later they moved out of Reception and Casey threw a sidelong glance at Adele. 'Does that suit you?' he asked.

'Oh, yes,' she said. 'I don't want to bring any charges against Elvira but, on the other hand, if it can be avoided I'd rather not have any further dealings with her.'

'That sounds sensible to me.' He paused as they reached his consulting room. 'I have a surgery to do now—how about you?'

'I'm going to grab a quick coffee then I'm doing a couple of house calls for Jeanette. She has a meeting with Ruby about counselling for Lara.'

'OK.' He nodded, and as she would have moved away he lightly touched her arm. 'I'll see you later.' He spoke softly so that only she would hear.

'Yes,' she whispered, with a thrill of anticipation. 'Of course.'

She felt as if she were walking on air as she made her way to the staffroom—she could still hardly believe what was happening to her. This heady feeling, this lurching of her heart whenever she caught sight of Casey, the torment when they were apart and the way he filled her thoughts in every waking moment were so unlike anything she had ever known before that sometimes she found herself dreading that it might all come to an end.

Pushing open the staffroom door, she almost ran into the room then she stopped in surprise because Celia Fletcher was sitting in the big chair by the window. With her long, slender legs crossed, she was flicking through the pages of a glossy magazine. It was so unusual to see the senior partner's wife at Woolverton House that for a moment Adele found herself lost for words.

Celia looked up. 'Adele, my dear!' she exclaimed. 'How are you?'

'I'm well, thank you, Celia.' She paused. 'This is a surprise, seeing you here.'

Celia smiled. 'I know. I have to confess I don't come here very much. I'm just waiting for Edward to finish his surgery. He's promised to take me to lunch.'

'Well, that's nice…'

'Actually, Adele…' Swiftly Celia interrupted her. 'I'm glad I've seen you. There was something I wanted to talk to you about.'

'Really?' Adele wondered what on earth the senior partner's wife and herself could possibly have in common.

'Edward tells me that you and Casey have been seeing each other lately.' Celia came straight to the point.

'Yes, that's true, we have,' Adele agreed. Guessing what might be coming next, she rushed on, 'It's all right. Edward didn't seem to think there would be a problem with Casey being my trainer, provided we're discreet and don't let anything interfere with our work…'

'Oh, I'm not worried about that,' said Celia with a dismissive little wave of her hand.

'No?'

'Not at all, and under normal circumstances I would be delighted for the pair of you. I love it when friends of ours get together. No, my worry is something else altogether. I became concerned when I first saw you, the night you came to dinner, but then I thought that you and Toby had something going and I stopped worrying. Later, however, Edward told me about you and Casey and it was then that I made up my mind I should warn you.'

'Warn me?' Adele frowned. 'Whatever do you mean?' A niggle of fear had started somewhere at the back of her mind, a fear that looked as if it could threaten her newly found happiness with Casey.

'You know that Casey was married before, don't you?' said Celia.

'Yes, of course,' Adele replied, 'and that his wife died—and his baby daughter.'

'I knew Casey at the time. I also knew his wife, Trisha—we all worked at the same hospital. Casey was devastated when it happened.'

'Yes, I'm sure he was.' Adele nodded in agreement, wondering just where this could be leading.

'The thing is, Adele, he hasn't been able to commit to anyone since. You see, he adored Trisha. Oh, there have been others since, one in particular, a lovely girl, another nurse, but Casey couldn't commit himself. He moved on—she was heartbroken.'

'Yes, but—'

'No, hear me out, Adele.' Celia raised her hand. 'This other girl was tall and dark-haired, just like Trisha...'

'Maybe that's simply the type Casey is attracted to.'

'Yes, probably so,' Celia agreed, 'but the thing is, Adele, not only are you that same type but you also happen to be the image of Trisha as well.'

'What?' Adele stared at Celia.

'It struck me the moment I met you. I couldn't believe my eyes. I thought I was seeing a ghost. Even your mannerisms are the same and the sound of your voice. Like I say, I feared for the situation then but when you appeared to be so taken with Toby I thought my fears were unfounded. But now I know the truth I really feel I should warn you before you get too attached to Casey. I would hate you to get hurt and, believe me, that's what will happen when Casey moves on again—because he will, make no mistake about that.'

*   *   *

'Before you get too attached to Casey,' Celia had said. If only she knew. Already it was too late. Adele was in as deep as it was possible to be. She loved him and she'd hoped he felt the same way about her. Celia's revelations had come as a shock and Adele knew she needed time to think. Pleading a headache that evening, she told Casey she intended having an early night. He seemed disappointed but so concerned about her that she ended up feeling guilty about lying to him.

In the time that she had known him Casey hadn't given the slightest indication that she resembled his late wife, but what Celia had told her offered a possible explanation for the strange expression on Casey's face when they'd first met and on other numerous occasions when she'd found him watching her. It also explained Celia's strange reaction on meeting her. But more worrying than that was that Celia had said Casey would use her as he had used others in some desperate quest to reconstruct the past then, when that failed, he would leave her and move on.

If that was how it was going to be, Adele knew deep in her heart that she should end the relationship now. After Nigel, she had vowed never to allow herself to become so involved with a man again unless the relationship carried some promise of commitment.

And had there been any such promise from Casey? With a little jolt she was forced to admit there hadn't. Caught up in the thrill of the affair, it had been easy to imagine a glorious future ahead of them, but when she really thought about it she had to accept the stark truth, and that was that Casey hadn't as much as mentioned the future.

Could it really be, as Celia had suggested, that he was living purely for the moment? Since his wife's death did he really find it impossible to love anyone else and was this why he'd wanted to keep their relationship as low-key as possible—because he knew it wasn't going to last?

He'd told her he loved her. Mostly, deep in the night as he made wonderful love to her, as they soared together or afterwards when he tenderly held her, he would tell her he loved her. But when he did so, was it her he was talking to or was it Trisha? Because she looked so like his dead wife, did he imagine it was Trisha he was making love to once more? The thought made her blood run cold and by the end of a sleepless night spent tossing and turning Adele knew she would have to confront Casey. If her fears proved to be true, she knew she would have no other choice but to end the relationship even though it would break her heart to do so.

The following day was extremely busy and she saw Casey only once in passing when he asked briefly if she was feeling better. Later, just as she was finishing her late afternoon surgery, her phone rang.

'Adele, it's me.' There was no need for him to explain— she would have known that voice anywhere. 'I have a police call-out. Care to come along?'

'Er, yes, of course.'

'You hesitate. Are you sure?'

'Yes, I'm sure.' She couldn't let her personal feelings stand in the way of her training, even though she wondered how she would cope in the future, working alongside Casey, if their relationship came to an end.

'We'll take the bike,' he said shortly. 'I'll meet you outside in five minutes.'

She flew up to her flat and changed into warm trousers and a thick sweater. Pulling on a padded jacket and gloves, she hurried down to the courtyard where she found Casey already astride the bike with its engine running. The spare crash helmet was on the pillion seat ready for her and within seconds she had put it on, secured it and had mounted the bike behind him. Then they were away and instinctively Adele wrapped her arms around Casey's waist, holding him tight as they sped to the police station. She could feel the warmth of his body through his jacket and beneath her the deep throbbing of the engine. It felt good to be there, good to be alive and good to be Casey's woman, and it was with a sudden painful pang that she remembered this could be about to come to end, for while the motorbike journeys might well continue, she might soon no longer be Casey's woman.

At the police station a harassed-looking Alan was on duty and briefly outlined the problem as he escorted them to an interview room. It appeared that a woman had been caught shoplifting by a store detective and the police had been called. The woman had been brought to the station where she had been charged, but during the bail process she had been taken ill.

'She looks pretty groggy,' said Alan.

'What age is she?' asked Casey.

'Sixty-five,' Alan replied.

'Does she have anyone with her?' asked Adele.

'Yes, her son has arrived but he seems more concerned with the shame and embarrassment of his mother having been arrested for shoplifting than over the fact that there might be something wrong with her.' As he finished outlining the details, Alan pushed open the door, allowing Casey and Adele to precede him into the interview room.

A grey-haired woman was seated in a chair with a red blanket around her shoulders. She looked pale and dazed and the right side of her face looked as if it had dropped, giving her a curiously lopsided appearance. A police-woman was crouched on one side of her and a man of around forty, dressed in an immaculate pinstriped suit, was pacing around the room. As the door opened he stopped pacing and spun round.

'Are you the doctor?' he demanded.

'Yes. The name's Casey and this is my assistant, Dr Brooks.'

'This is my mother,' the man went on. 'There must have been some dreadful mistake. They're saying she was caught shoplifting but that's impossible—she wouldn't do anything like that. The last thing she would want is to bring shame on the family—on me, in my position.'

'And what is your position, Mr…Mr…?' asked Adele as Casey crouched down in front of the woman in the chair.

'Lauder. Robert Lauder. I'm chairman of the local council. I also have my own firm of accountants. I tell you, all this is simply ludicrous.'

Casey spoke quietly to the woman in the chair. 'Mrs Lauder, can you tell me what happened?'

The woman stared at him but when she attempted to speak her words sounded garbled.

'Good Lord!' Robert Lauder, who had been staring down at his mother, now ran one hand over his head in distraction. 'You haven't been drinking again, have you, Mother? Heaven help us!' He rolled his eyes then turned to Adele. 'She's always been a bit partial to the sherry bottle, but I didn't think she'd get into this state. On the other hand, I suppose it might account for her actions in the store. I mean…if she was drunk…'

By this time Casey had checked Mrs Lauder's pulse and shone his torch into her eyes.

'Is that it, Doctor? Is she drunk?' demanded Robert. He sounded hopeful now, as if it had just occurred to him that this possibility could be by far the lesser of two evils.

'I just want to check your mother's blood pressure,' replied Casey. Adele recognised the cool note in his voice and knew he didn't think much of the man's attitude. As Casey took a sphygmomanometer from his bag, she helped him to expose the patient's arm and secure the cuff. As he checked the pressure she looked up at the patient's son once more.

'Does your mother live alone?' she asked.

'Yes, since my father died—that was two years ago.' Robert spoke as if that should have been a sufficient length of time for his mother to be over her bereavement. 'So...' He looked at Casey who had removed the cuff and straightened up. 'Am I right? Too much sherry?'

'No, Mr Lauder,' Casey replied. 'Your mother has suffered a stroke.'

'A stroke!' Robert looked astounded.

'Yes, it has affected her right side and she's suffered some paralysis and loss of speech. I want to get her admitted to hospital right away.' He turned to Alan who was still standing by the door. 'Can you arrange an ambulance, please, Sergeant?'

'Of course, Doctor,' Alan replied.

'He's a bit of a monster, the son,' said Adele as they stood on the forecourt and watched the ambulance draw away, bearing Robert Lauder and his mother.

'We mustn't judge him too harshly,' said Casey as he put on his crash helmet and passed Adele hers. 'All he could see was his life becoming complicated.'

'But she's his mother!' protested Adele.

'I know, and on the face of it his treatment of her did seem pretty uncaring, but we don't know all the facts, Adele, and ours is not to reason why.'

In silence Adele mounted the bike, but as they drew away from the station inside she was still seething.

They had travelled for several miles before she realised that they were nowhere near Woolverton House. She leaned forward. 'Where are we going?' she shouted. When Casey didn't answer she thought her words must have been whipped away by the speed at which they were travelling, but a few moment later he pulled into what seemed to be a lay-by and switched off the engine.

Looking around, Adele saw they were on a fairly deserted road high above the town. By now it was late afternoon and the sun was sinking fast in the glorious blush of a mackerel sky while below them smoke from several fires drifted upwards in long thin columns.

Casey indicated for her to dismount. Doing the same himself, he took her hand and said, 'I want to show you something.'

Mystified, she allowed him to lead her through a gap in the hedge and into a field. Below them against the dramatic skyline were the ruins of the once magnificent Stourborne Abbey, to their left lay the town, slumbering in the last of the day's sunlight, and beyond the sweep of the distant hills.

'That,' said Casey as he slipped his arm around her, 'is one magnificent view, do you not agree?'

'Yes,' Adele agreed, 'it is.'

'I've always wanted to live somewhere with such a view,' Casey went on.

'It would be marvellous.' Adele nodded, wondering why Casey had brought her here.

'Actually,' he said after a moment, 'some of this land up here is about to be developed and I'm thinking of putting a deposit on one of the plots. But if I'm to do so I need to move fast—I imagine they'll be snapped up immediately.'

'Yes, I imagine they would.' This didn't come as any

great surprise—Adele had known that Casey was only staying in his flat at Woolverton House until he found a new property.

'The thing is, Adele…' his arm tightened around her. 'I don't want to do so unless I'm sure that it's what you would want as well.'

'Me?' Slowly she half turned to him, for a moment unable to take in what he was saying.

'Yes.' Suddenly his voice sounded husky. 'I'm sorry, I didn't mean to rush you over this. I know we said we'd take things slowly but this opportunity has come up…' He trailed off.

'You mean you want to have a house built up here and you want me to move in with you?' She could hardly believe what she was hearing. This sounded nothing like the Casey who wouldn't allow himself to commit to anyone.

'What I would really like is for us to be married,' he said softly. Turning to face her, he looked down into her eyes. 'There… I've said it and I really am rushing you now, I know, so maybe if you'd prefer it we could live together first…'

'No, oh, no!'

'No?' His face fell.

'Oh, what I mean is yes.' She stared up at him as a wave of pure happiness washed over her. 'Oh, Casey, of course I'll marry you.'

'You will?' He looked astounded and delighted at the same time. 'I thought it was far too soon but I have to say I was getting fed up with keeping it quiet from everyone.'

'What about Edward, and you being my trainer and everything?'

'I shouldn't think there will be any objection. Fiancée has a much more respectable, if old-fashioned ring to it than live-in lover. And when your training is over I imagine the others will finally see the need for another partner—always supposing that's what you want, of course,' he added hastily.

'I may want to concentrate on police work.'

'Whatever.' He shrugged.

'Or have lots of babies.'

'Wonderful.' His arm tightened around her. 'Even better. And I don't think we need have any fears about Edward. I'm sure he will be delighted. Celia, too,' he added with a chuckle.

'Celia?' Adele looked up at him quickly. She had planned to confront him over what Celia had told her but now she wondered whether it was necessary. Celia's fear had been that he would be incapable of committing to her, but surely there was no greater commitment than a proposal of marriage?

'Celia has been wanting me to settle down again for years. But I kept telling her you can only settle down with the right person.' He paused and lightly touched her cheek. 'After I lost Trisha I despaired of ever finding that right person again. I tried dating one or two but I think it must have been too soon after Trisha…and then…and then you walked into my life, Adele, and I knew instantly. The moment I met you, I knew you were the person I wanted to spend the rest of my life with.'

'Am I like Trisha at all?' She spoke lightly but her heart was thumping as she waited for his reply.

Casey frowned. 'A bit, I suppose,' he said at last, 'in some ways, but in others not at all. You are you, Adele, and it's you who I want for my wife.' Lowering his head, his lips covered hers in a kiss both tender and full of passion. Her earlier fears melted away, leaving her in no doubt about his intentions or the depth of his love.

'There is just one question,' she said as at last she drew away from him.

'Oh?' he murmured. 'And what's that?'

'While this house is being built, while I'm your fiancée, can we be live-in lovers?'

'Oh,' he said, his arms tightening around her, 'I'm sure that can be arranged.'

'Well, that's all right, then.' She gave a little sigh of pure contentment and, lifting her arms, wound them around his neck. 'Because I'm not sure I could wait for as long as it takes to build a house.'

Modern Romance™
...seduction and
passion guaranteed

Tender Romance™
...love affairs that
last a lifetime

Sensual Romance™
...sassy, sexy and
seductive

Blaze
...sultry days and
steamy nights

Medical Romance™
...medical drama on
the pulse

Historical Romance™
...rich, vivid and
passionate

27 new titles every month.

*With all kinds of Romance for
every kind of mood...*

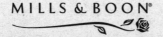

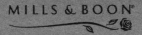

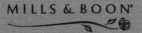

Don't miss *Book Four* of this BRAND-NEW 12 book collection 'Bachelor Auction'.

Who says money can't buy love?

On sale 6th December

FREE!

2 Books
and a surprise gift!

We would like to take this opportunity to thank you for reading this Mills & Boon® book by offering you the chance to take TWO more specially selected titles from the Medical Romance™ series absolutely FREE! We're also making this offer to introduce you to the benefits of the Reader Service™ —

- ★ FREE home delivery
- ★ FREE gifts and competitions
- ★ FREE monthly Newsletter
- ★ Books available before they're in the shops
- ★ Exclusive Reader Service discount

Accepting these FREE books and gift places you under no obligation to buy; you may cancel at any time, even after receiving your free shipment. Simply complete your details below and return the entire page to the address below. *You don't even need a stamp!*

YES! Please send me 2 free Medical Romance books and a surprise gift. I understand that unless you hear from me, I will receive 4 superb new titles every month for just £2.55 each, postage and packing free. I am under no obligation to purchase any books and may cancel my subscription at any time. The free books and gift will be mine to keep in any case.

M2ZEB

Ms/Mrs/Miss/Mr ....Initials..
BLOCK CAPITALS PLEASE

Surname...

Address..

....

....Postcode ....

Send this whole page to:
UK: The Reader Service, FREEPOST CN81, Croydon, CR9 3WZ
EIRE: The Reader Service, PO Box 4546, Kilcock, County Kildare (stamp required)

Offer not valid to current Reader Service subscribers to this series. We reserve the right to refuse an application and applicants must be aged 18 years or over. Only one application per household. Terms and prices subject to change without notice. Offer expires 28th February 2003. As a result of this application, you may receive offers from Harlequin Mills & Boon and other carefully selected companies. If you would prefer not to share in this opportunity please write to The Data Manager at the address above.

Mills & Boon® is a registered trademark owned by Harlequin Mills & Boon Limited.
Medical Romance™ is being used as a trademark.